CW00456662

LOST AND FOUND

THE EVIE CHESTER FILES: CASE 1

NITA ROUND

Edited by
KRISTA WALSH

Cover design
MAY DAWNEY

PINK
TEA
BOOKS

Copyright © 2020 by Nita Round

All rights reserved.

The right of Nita Round to be identified as the author of this work has been asserted by her in accordance with the Copyright, Patents and Design Act 1988.

No part of this book may be reproduced in any form or by any electronic or mechanical means, including information storage and retrieval systems, without written permission from the author, except for the use of brief quotations in a book review.

The characters, incidents and dialogue herein are fictional and any resemblance to actual events or persons, living or dead, is purely coincidental.

To Amy Herman-Pall
Thank you for all of your help and hard work

———————

To my wife.
Evie's here!

Thank you for choosing to read this book.

Evie Chester grew out of a writers convention held in Bristol, UK. She started life as a short story but soon grew into something much more. She's featured as a secondary character in a couple of the Towers novels, but her place is greater now than the sum of her parts.
This is a new series and you don't need to read any Tower books first.

I hope you enjoy this story and read the rest of her case files. If you like the world, take a look at the other books in the Towers of the Earth universe.

https://www.nitaround.com

Copyright © 2020 by Nita Round. All rights reserved.

1

The first time Evie Chester saw the woman, she thought she was a man. Tall and imposing, she planted herself as though she had every right to be there. Shoulders stiff, back straight, and pale serious eyes that seemed to watch everything all at once. Nothing escaped her attention.

She wore a fine suit. A simple cut, not too fancy but well made, with a white shirt that very nearly shone. A dark bowler covered unfashionably short blonde hair. Underneath her jacket, she wore a pale green buttoned vest with decorative silk work and a pale green cravat. She appeared a rather well-to-do gent. All in all, she had no place here in the middle of the smelly, dirty docks, surrounded by the men of the quayside with their coarse dress and coarser manners.

At her side stood another woman, and whilst the first woman was all light and bright, this one was darker. She was also tall for a woman, with dark hair, dark eyes, and a permanent smile upon her face. She wore leather clothing like some distant native of a far distant land. Oddest of all, she carried a sword on her back. Who in their right mind would advertise they duelled with a sword? A woman, too. Odd. Independent. Strange. Free. They were free, and she was not.

Seeing them made her despise her lack of freedom, which made her place in the world even darker.

Left to her own devices, Evie would never have known of their existence, but like the two women, Harold, her *escort* for the day, had stopped to listen to Iskabard Speare. Harold wanted to listen to everything he said. Maybe for the promise of work or the chance to learn how to get rich quick, like Iskabard claimed. None of it mattered to Evie; all she wanted was to gawk at the woman who looked like a man. Her companion, too, for she was also an unusual sight in Bristelle.

"Friends," Iskabard called out over the noise of the gathering crowd. "I have a new design. One that will turn long-distance travel on its head." He waved a roll of paper like a wand. "The propellers of the future will move the dirigibles and blimps at speeds beyond that of even the fastest ocean liner. We see the future of air travel opening even further, and we, the ship builders of Bristelle, want to be a part of that future."

The crowd made appreciative noises to his claims.

"Once, we built ocean-going ships of every size, here in these very docks. But those days have gone. When the time of the airships came, we adjusted. Alas, there are always other yards and docks, and we've lost much of our shipbuilding to other regions in recent years. That will change, my friends, I promise you. We will regain our place amongst the greatest shipyards of the world."

There were cheers at this statement. They liked this.

"We will rebuild our business here in Bristelle with new ships and new propellers. Once more, we will be the greatest shipbuilders in the whole of the world."

Now the crowd roared their approval, and there were a great many people to add their voices. The lure of fine words and the promise of work made many men, and their long-suffering wives, happy.

"Girl," Harold said. "We need to go now." He didn't wait

for her answer. He wrapped his thick hand around her arm and pulled so hard she almost fell over.

Evie wanted to tell him that she wasn't a girl, she was a woman. Yet she dared not speak for fear of an even greater reprimand.

"Come on, you stupid good-for-nothing tart, don't make a scene. We've work to do," he said.

Evie gritted her teeth. If anyone did any work, it was her. Not that she would ever allude to it. The last time she'd even come close to saying so, he'd punched her right at the top of her arm where the bruise would not show. Her arm had probably bruised under his grip already without her adding to the damage.

He half dragged Evie to a warehouse on the southern edge of the quay. A little way beyond the warehouse, the lifting platforms stood quiet. Little cargo moved from the river to the canals these days, and the mechanisms stood rusting. This was yet another symptom of the prosperity that no longer flowed into Bristelle.

Quiet and rundown, the warehouse was a good place for the kind of business Harold conducted. A cobbled street extended the full length of the building and all the way back into the heart of Bristelle. Several small carriages stood to one side, their drivers huddled in their seats waiting to be recalled to duty. It wasn't far to walk to the warehouse doors from where the carriages were. Perish the thought that the gents of the city had to muddy their nice shoes in the filth of the working man. Thirty yards in front of the warehouse ran the river itself. Riverboats berthed right outside the warehouse, too.

Harold knocked on the door. Three solid bangs, a pause, followed by two more bangs.

"Who's there?" asked a voice from inside.

"Jed, open the damned door, you bloody fool. It's me, Harold."

The door opened wide, and Jed, with black hair, pale skin, and protruding teeth, stood in the doorway.

"Dat's her?" he asked. "She don't look much. Are yer sure?"

"Yeah, yeah, course I'm sure. She cost me more than enough," Harold replied.

Jed reached out and touched her hair. "A blonde one. Them ain't common."

Evie flinched at his touch, but there was nothing she could do; Harold maintained his ironlike grip on her arm and wouldn't let her get far.

"Can she speak? You know, like a normal?" Jed asked.

"What, you mean can she speak Anglish? She's cursed, not a moron, you idiot. Now let us inside so we can get our business sorted. We don't need any attention."

"There are loads waiting. They've been gathering all morning," Jed said.

"Good, and you charged them all a silver shilling for the privilege of being seen by the girl?"

"Aye, I did. And I gave 'em all a token like you said."

"I'm not a girl," Evie said.

"Lookee that, she got a right funny accent," Jed said.

"Talk of the kettle calling the pot black," Evie said. He spoke with the slow lilt of the out-of-city farmer and sounded quite slow himself.

Harold pinched her arm to keep her quiet. "And did you warn them that any odd requests would cost extra?"

"I did. I ain't no fool," Jed replied. "What do you mean by odd requests, though?"

Harold didn't answer that one. "Good chap, Jed. We'll be rich," he said instead. "Well, we will so long as we earn more than she cost us." He dragged Evie inside. "Come on in, girl," he said, as though she had a choice in the matter.

She tried to drag her heels to delay the inevitable, but that didn't deter him.

He stopped and turned to her. "Hey, are you gonna be awkward or what?"

Evie glared at him; it was her only way to express defiance. She was called Gifted, but her 'gift' amounted to a curse, and the value of her life lay only in her ability to use it when it was demanded of her. As such, her worth in the world amounted to very little. The sheep in the fields had more value than she did, a fact she'd grasped from a very young age.

"I own you today," Harold said, "and you will do as you are told." The threat in his words didn't need to be spoken aloud; Evie heard it clearly enough.

"I understand," she replied.

Inside the entrance, she let her eyes take in the vastness of the warehouse. Like a barn, it was a shell of a building, with wooden floors and an open-arched roof two storeys above.

Harold glanced at the crowd gathered. There must have been a hundred men here. At a schilling a piece, Evie realised Harold would probably cover the money she'd cost him and still have plenty of profit. Her chances of surviving the day had gone up.

Jed picked up a cudgel that stood against the wall. He banged it hard against the door frame. "Listen up," he said.

Harold took over. "It's your lucky day. No matter what you got, we got a cure. Form a line, and the girl will see you one at a time. When you come up, show me your token else you ain't seeing no one, and Jed here will add to your problems."

He grabbed Evie's arm and dragged her to the far corner where two spindly chairs stood next to an equally rickety table. A small brass pot sat on the floor.

"This will do," he said. He turned to face the sea of expectant faces. "Roll up, roll up. Show me your token. Who's first?"

A ruddy-faced chap, better dressed than most, came to

stand next to them. They'd all paid to have their ailments cured, but still, the touch of a gifted was not one that many looked forward to.

"Token," Harold said.

The ruddy-faced man gave him the token, and Harold stared at it for a few moments. He nodded and threw the token into the pot. "One token, one cure, got it?"

The man swallowed and came closer. He swallowed so hard his whole face shuddered.

"Show me," Evie said.

He turned an even brighter shade of red. "I thought it would be private," he said.

Evie smiled. He seemed quite a pleasant chap, really, and actually stuttered as he spoke. "It's all right, sweetie. Is it . . . you know?" She stared at his groin and hoped he got the idea.

He nodded.

"Clap, crabs, the wiener pox, fleas, or something else?"

"I . . . I . . ."

Evie grabbed his hand. "Steady on and relax." She stared into his eyes; sometimes it helped them to settle. At the moment, he had the aspect of a scared rabbit about ready to run or fall over.

"You have lovely eyes," he said.

Evie didn't reply to the comment. Nice eyes or not, she was owned; nice eyes didn't help her in any way. Harold, or rather people like him, didn't need the niceties, they needed her to get on with things.

She closed her eyes and stared at the sickness that ate him. "Does it itch and burn?" she asked.

He nodded.

Evie swallowed, and the tang of his sickness filled her mouth. This time, the aroma and the flavour of curdled milk coated her tongue. She tried not to show her level of distaste as she tasted the disease in him. Her gift, sampled his blight and the disease crawled through his hands into hers. Where they touched, her skin burned, and it did not stop until her gift thought her done.

Hand to hand was not always the best way. It hurt more for a start. It seemed as though she sucked at the darkness like a vacuum device, and that added a kind of pressure as the taint raced into her own body. It was easier when she touched the sickness itself, because it would jump into her more easily, smoothly, and with far less pain. Of course, none of these men would want to drop their breeches in such a public place. To be fair, Evie didn't want them to do that either.

This was her gift. To take the sickness from another and draw it inside herself. A cure to them, and nothing but vileness to her.

She pulled her hands from his when she'd finished. "It's done. Go home. Wash the area in salted water, and you'll be a man to your wife again. No itches either."

"Thank you, thank you," he said. He obviously felt better, because he threw a farthing onto the table. Harold grinned; all yellow teeth and cracked lips. He'd probably not anticipated gratuities. Evie hadn't either, but from her experience, one should never underestimate a grateful man.

She moved on to the next *client*. As soon as she cured one person, another stepped forward to take his place. One after the other.

She wondered why these men didn't watch where they stuck it, because that seemed to be the only kind of sickness she had to deal with. It wasn't her place to say so, but at least one of them had to have worked out the cause and effect. She shrugged off the thought. She had work to do.

After a dozen clients, she was almost at her limit. Not quite, but very close. She thought of herself as a sponge, absorbing the rot from people, but even a sponge had its saturation point. Now she needed to purge all that she had absorbed, and like a sponge, she had to wring herself dry of taint.

"Harold, it's time," she said.

He took a swig from his small hip flask. "Time? What time? Shut up and do your thing."

"You were advised of my needs before you took me. Now I need a screen and a bucket."

"Shut up and get on wi'it."

"All right, then," she said. "Next."

A half dozen more forgettable faces followed, but the line of men never seemed to diminish. Thankfully for Evie, they were all minor illness, but that didn't mean she was able to do much more. She needed a rest, and she needed time to purge and recover.

She took one look at the next man in line and discerned that this was one who needed more than she had left to give right then and there. A shadow twirled inside him, wrapped itself around his backbone, and narrow tendrils of darkness speared through his skull.

There was nothing she could do to help him in her current state. She was done and full. She needed a rest and a chance to replace her energy levels. She glared at Harold, and he scowled back at her.

Tired, hungry, and with no end in sight, despair welled up. Even though she had no rights as a person, she still felt things.

Evie turned to Harold and ignored his glower. "Please, I need a bucket and a screen. Also water and food. Do you have them?"

"I tol' ya once already, just shut your mouth and get on wi'it," he said.

He gave her no choice.

"All right. Have it your way." She purged right there. Right in front of the next punter. It wasn't a pleasant sight. The sickness gathered under her skin and darkened. Not like the dark skins of Frika, but her light skin filled with a black shapes like lacework. Sickness like drops of oil gathered at the ends of her fingers and oozed around her fingernails.

Drops splattered to the ground and seeped into the planks of the warehouse floor. It wasn't only that she splattered the floor, but that purge stank. All of the sickness from all of the men concentrated into black tar.

Something vile welled into her mouth, and she spat out large glob of green and yellow phlegm. The taste of it almost turned her stomach, but better out than in.

Harold remained sat in his rickety chair, his mouth open. Shock, perhaps? Or because he knew that with a mouth open, he didn't need to take in the stench of what had erupted from her body. Evie didn't care.

Some of the paying customers were not so enthused at her display, but she was unable to do anything about that.

"What the fuck is this?" Harold asked.

Evie coughed a couple of times to clear her throat. "I said I needed to purge, and this is it. I asked for a screen, and you refused, so everyone gets to see the results of their dark diseases." She doubled over and vomited under the table. She missed his feet, but only just. Not that he would have noticed; he didn't exactly wear the finest footwear to start with.

She wiped her mouth as she stood up. His fist caught her at the side of the face with such force that Evie spun around and ended up on the floor. She missed her own vomit by an inch.

She ran her tongue over her teeth and felt one loosen, and the bone in her jaw was cracked. She lay on the floor and touched her face; it would heal, but broken bones were a bitch to fix.

Harold, however, didn't care. He radiated rage.

"Stop it, Harold," Jed said. Strange how the simpleton was the one to stop the beating she expected. "You have

9

customers. We can't be giving them their money back. Not now."

That stopped him, and Evie knew Harold and Jed needed this more than she needed to comply. They could beat her, but too much and they would incur the wrath of her owner, Godwyn Bethwood. He would happily starve and beat his property, but woe betide anyone who thought to abuse anything of his.

Jed helped Evie to her feet.

"You were told," she said. Her words were slurred from the face damage. "I need food. Water. A screen and a bucket in which to purge."

The anger still blazed in Harold's eyes.

"You see what happens if I can't purge, and the food and water will keep me alive whilst I do it. Should I sicken, there will be more hell to pay."

"I'll get it. Food, drink, a screen," Jed said.

"Thank you," Evie said. It hurt to talk with her jaw cracked. The food would help speed up the healing process, at least.

Harold nodded. "And see if you can get the ones who ran away to come back. No refunds anyway." Harold handed Jed a couple of sixpence pieces. "Get me some ale as well."

Jed shrugged and left.

Harold stared at her, and his eyes slid to the men who were closest. His feral grin looked frightening and real. "I think it'd be best to move the work area to one that doesn't stink. You know what these filthy cursed ones are like." He winked at the men still in line, and they nodded as though they agreed. Given the mess on the floor, she probably hadn't shown her best side. Even so, Harold still spoke a load of shit. She didn't want to push things by telling him so. Survival first, that was the best she could hope for.

After they moved positions, while they waited for Jed to return, Harold forced her to see to the men. "Come on, chaps.

Let her take the shit from inside you. Let her be the one to suffer. This is what she's for. Step up. Who's next?"

When Jed returned, he brought with him ale for each of them. The food was basic, but good enough to sustain her as she worked through the day until the light beyond the warehouse windows grew dim and the shadows across the floor grew longer.

Evie had seen and healed three quarters of the men who had gathered here that morning, and she was exhausted. Yet the line of men still waiting seemed almost as long as when she'd started. Her heart sank. Every time she healed someone, another person joined the queue. She viewed the line of expectant faces and sighed. What was the point? Death would be better than this. The crowd always considered Evie with barely disguised distrust. Even when she made them feel better. As a Gifted woman, she would be the devil to blame for all the misfortunes in their lives. Such despair filled her heart that she did not notice when the atmosphere inside the warehouse changed.

Harold jumped to his feet and stood with his hands on his hips, and his sudden movement caught Evie's attention.

"Good afternoon," said a voice. A feminine voice, but one filled with certainty and strength. "Stop what you're doing."

"Who the fuck are you?" he asked, his voice laced with incredulity.

"A concerned citizen," the woman answered. "I hear you're abusing a woman. I can't allow that."

"And what the hell are you gonna do about it?" Harold bellowed.

"Stop you," she answered.

Harold laughed, but the men in the room didn't join him. They quietened down and shuffled out of the way. Many of them were not the sort who sought a fight, unlike Jed and Harold. Footsteps, two sets, echoed in the vastness of the warehouse.

"And before anyone gets any ideas, my companion here is a very capable swordswoman," she said.

Evie looked up. It was them. The blonde who looked like a man and the sword-wielding woman wearing leathers. The swordswoman had her blade out, and she grinned, as though she rather liked the idea of violence and swordplay.

"Who the hell are you?" Harold asked.

The blonde woman didn't answer. Instead, she strode over to Evie and knelt at her side. "Are you all right?" Her pale grey eyes stared at Evie as though she saw into her soul to the pain that lived there.

"Tired," Evie replied.

"I expect so. What are they doing to you?" She reached out, and long fingers brushed against the side of her face where the bruise probably showed. "Actually, you don't need to answer right now."

"You mustn't touch me," Evie said.

"No matter. I'm Magda Stoner, and my friend here is Ascara. We'll put a stop to this."

Harold huffed and puffed at the interruption. "Why don't you two freaks fuck off out of here? I don't think you noticed you're a little outnumbered."

Magda turned to her companion. "What do you think?"

"I think I can manage, but if you want to join in, then they're in big trouble."

"I thought so, too," Magda answered.

All the men stepped backwards, getting well away from the women.

"Fuck off. She's my property, at least for today, and she needs to earn her keep."

Magda rose to her feet. "What did you say?" she asked. "You own her? Like a slave? You are aware the Angles have laws about such things?"

"She's a cursed one; she has no rights. Either owned or dead, take your pick." To show his position on the issue of

Evie's freedom, he punched her in the side of the head. He seemed to like using his fists on people who couldn't or wouldn't fight back.

"Magda, let me deal with this one," said Ascara. "Please. Let me."

"Oh no, you had the last one."

"Are you keeping score?" Ascara shrugged. "Fine. If you insist."

"What the hell are you doing?" Harold asked.

Magda removed her jacket and hat. Now it was easier to see that she was no man. She rolled back the cuffs of her shirt and grinned. "I think you hit this woman for no reason, didn't you?"

"She ain't a woman, she's a thing," Harold replied.

"Would you like to try that fist against me?"

Harold snorted. "A woman is a woman."

"Some people never learn, Magda," Ascara said.

"I know," Magda replied.

She punched him in the nose, so hard she heard it break. Blood gushed everywhere.

Evie stared with mouth open. She wasn't sure whether to be horrified or happy that someone, a woman, had done to him what he so readily did to others.

"He's a stupid man, Magda. He might need another lesson," Ascara said.

Magda flexed her hand. "You're right." Her next punch took him on the side of the face with such force he hit the ground with a thud.

Ascara kicked him over. "I think he needs to—"

As the sound of running feet drew closer, Ascara turned in time to see Jed with his cudgel.

"Idiot," she said. She sidestepped his clumsy swing and punched him in the face.

He folded over, blood dripping over his chin. "Ouch. You broke my nose," he moaned.

"Be thankful. Ascara here likes to collect male janglies. She prefers to rip them off with her hands, but she also has a sword so she can do it faster," Magda said.

"Right," said Jed. He backed away.

Magda faced those remaining. "Gentlemen, there is no further show for today. We will not tolerate the abuse of anyone, regardless of who they are. I suggest you go home and try not to get into any trouble."

She turned to Evie. "Are you Gifted?"

Evie nodded.

"I would ask you your gift, but it is not really my business, not if you don't want to speak of it."

Evie had never had the option to speak for herself before. "I can make people feel better," she replied.

Ascara grinned. "Sounds wonderful. I like women who can make me feel better."

"Ascara!" Magda admonished.

Ascara laughed.

"Well, can you at least share your name with us?" Magda asked.

Evie paused for a moment. If the likes of Harold were allowed to use her name, then who was she to refuse the two women who had saved her from more abuse?

"Evie," she said, "Evie Chester. I'm a slave here in Bristelle."

Magda smiled and offered her hand. "You *were* a slave, Evie Chester, now you are not. Come with us. We can offer you sanctuary, a place where we can introduce you to others, or we can take you some place safe. Keep your gift private or share it, it's your choice."

Evie stared at the outstretched hand as though Magda would snatch it away the moment she reached out.

Magda smiled. "Take my hand, and one day we will earn your trust well enough that you will never doubt me when I offer it."

2

_____

E vie Chester had not, even in her wildest dreams, expected to find herself living at number seventeen, Ardmore Street. In fact, Evie Chester had never expected to live in a house at all. Ever.

The landlady, Mrs Agatha Hickman, kept a good house: clean, warm, and dry. The furniture may have been old and well used, but it was better than she'd had in years. She was a friendly lady who didn't pry and always offered a smile, a cup of tea, and a kind word. Evie liked her.

Ardmore, was not the finest district in all of Bristelle, but it wasn't the slums either. People of all social classes walked the streets in comparative safety, and no one bothered the people in their fine clothes. Leastways, not during the hours of daylight, and as long as they stayed on the major streets, they were safe at night, too. Usually.

Here she was, living in style after she'd escaped her old life. To Evie Chester, it didn't matter that the furnishings were old and worn. As far as she was concerned, she was living in the lap of luxury.

It was the simple things that meant most. She had a room to call her own, with her own bed and enough blankets to keep her warm. She had a washstand with fresh water, and if she needed the water warmed, she just had to ask her landlady for it.

Best of all, and even more importantly, she had the freedom to come and go as she pleased.

This was freedom, and *freedom* took some getting used to. In the beginning, she'd been so scared of being caught again that she didn't leave her room for three days. She'd locked herself in and managed with the meagre food rations she'd taken with her. She had a few coins, but she didn't rush to spend them.

The first time she'd left the house, she'd raced to a nearby store, bought a small quarter tin loaf. It had cost ha'penny for something a little longer than her hand. She'd raced back to her rooms so fast she couldn't recall breathing the whole of the way.

It took another week before she'd become adventurous enough to find a tea house and sit in public. After that, and filled with confidence, she'd gone out whenever she wanted. She found a small teashop and diner near the docks. The customers were dockers and char-women, so the prices were cheap and within her price range. When she located the market, she bought more luxuries, like cheese.

These riches of coin, warmth, and food were more than she'd ever imagined. At the same time, she couldn't help but worry. The coins she had wouldn't last indefinitely, and her current good fortune wouldn't last forever. After she'd been rescued, she should have left the city, but it didn't feel right. Where would she have gone? Magda and Ascara had helped her find a place to live and funds enough to live well enough for a while at least.

Money was not her only concern. Evie needed to be careful of what she did and who saw her. She was an escaped slave after all. There were people on the streets of Bristelle who were no friends of hers. Those were the ones she needed to avoid. If only she knew who they were.

Every time someone glanced in her direction, she wondered if they were searching for her. Was her dress too shabby, and did it attract attention? Had she failed to wear her hair in the correct manner? Was the man next to the grocer browsing or waiting? Or waiting for her? Did that street kid loitering at the street corner stare at her a little too long?

Each journey beyond her front door brought with it a world of peril. Evie had to look at each and every person she passed in case she knew them. It was so hard to keep track of all of the faces in her mind. Every person might be her enemy, a spy, someone out to get her.

A sense of foreboding filled every waking moment, and Evie spent less time out on the street and more time in her room. She'd had such confidence, but her boldness had lasted only a short while. The risks of being found weighed on her too heavily and she could no longer fully enjoy her new-found freedom.

She stood to one side of the narrow sash window, much as she had done every day for the last fortnight, and peered around the edge of the thin curtains. Through the grime-encrusted glass, she looked down into the street two storeys below.

Evie wiped the window with a small piece of cloth, but the grime, which clouded the outside and not the inside of the pane, remained unaffected by her efforts. The dirt covered glass and the half-open curtains were all that stood between her and the rest of the world.

Outside, the sun shone with the hopefulness of spring turning to the heat of summer. Yet half of the street stood in the shade cast by the terraced houses of Ardmore Street. The road itself was easily wide enough for two carriages to pass, and the pavements were broad and paved. Ardmore Street was a busy throughway, and much traffic thundered along from the docks to the city and back again.

Above the tops of the houses, an airship, one of those huge cargo ones, flew overhead. The whole room reverberated with the thudding *thwomp* of the huge propellers as they powered the ship through the sky. This one headed towards the docks where the main cargo distribution centres stood. Evie knew about those. People like her always did. It was where all cargo transferred from the air to the canal, the rail, the river, and the road networks.

The smaller ships and dirigibles used by passengers headed to a different station. Bristelle Central Terminus stood some miles south and west of Ardmore. A well-to-do area by all accounts. Those who could afford to travel by air were not the sort who tolerated being lumped in with the dirty cargo, the stinky docks, or the plain folk who operated them.

Evie sighed at the sight of the airship; she had often wondered what it would be like to fly high in the sky. She imagined staring through the windows of the gondola as the ship soared above the world. She wondered, too, what it would be like to watch the clouds roll by like fields of snow.

Dreams. Such thoughts were nothing more than dreams. Silly, childhood dreams that were for other people and not for the likes of her. She needed to put them back in the past where they belonged and focus her attention, and her hopes, on more realistic goals. Like watching the people in the street.

She saw fine ladies with long, well-made skirts and matching jackets. She admired their frilly blouses, which looked finely made and expensive. Too expensive for her.

Even more spectacular, to Evie's eyes, were the hats. Some wore formal designs of dark and shiny satins, or more casual ones bedecked with bright and merry-coloured ribbons. One lady had a fascinator like a bird's nest covered in huge bright feathers and perched at such a precarious angle that it threatened to slide right off her head. It didn't, though, and she walked along the street with such a smooth and graceful step, she looked as though she floated.

Some of the men wore formal suits and hats, too, but their colours were muted and serious. They were well-dressed gents, for sure, possibly even professional gents who worked in offices with long names and bursting with importance. Or these posh gents may have had nothing better to do than seek entertainments wherever they could be found.

Others strolled the streets. These men were not gents, not by any stretch. Dressed in work clothes, they seemed rough. They paraded along the walkways in the way of men who knew how to take care of themselves. These men were trouble, and they would find even more trouble in any one of the public houses down the side streets.

The pride of Ardmore, though, was not a pub, but the gin palace that stood at the corner of Pump Street, a stone's throw away. There were no signs above the door, but people knew what it was, and that place drew more attention than any other drinking establishment.

Evie started to turn away. A day, like any other day, with nothing more to worry about.

And that was when she saw him.

Fingers of ice gripped her heart and squeezed until she could barely breathe. She wanted to run away and hide, or let the earth open up and swallow her. Either option seemed like a good one.

She backed away from the window until she bumped against the end of the bed and dropped onto the mattress. She grabbed hold of the bedstead and held on as though her life depended upon it. For those precious moments, it did.

Time passed. A minute or an hour, or as long as it took for Evie to remember how to breathe. When she did, she gulped down the air as though she had almost drowned. Courage found her then, and she rose to her feet. Slow and tentative steps took her back to the window so that she peered around the edges of the curtain into the street once more.

There he was, still there on the opposite side of the street. A tall and gangly fellow, all hunched as he worked to appear less conspicuous. He leaned against the wall with his hands shoved deep into his trouser pockets. His jacket looked certain to fit a much larger man, and his hat sat at a jaunty angle to obscure his face. There was something about him that spooked her.

He glared at everyone who walked by, and Evie recognised that glare even from this distance. She didn't know him by name but knew him well enough to recognise who he worked for. That man on the street was one of Godwyn Bethwood's men.

At the mere thought of the name Bethwood, her heart rate increased until it pounded in her chest like a beast trying to escape. She'd almost allowed herself to forget what it was like to be caged.

They'd found her. Or they were close to finding her. They would not have a man outside if they weren't sure of where she was.

She shivered as the terror of being hunted rose through her like a shower of cold water. The thought that they were so close, that they'd catch her and she'd be forced to return to the life she'd escaped, filled her with horror. Her knees turned to jelly, and she wasn't sure she could stand for much longer.

They say the difference between life and death is no more than a fine line. One glance at that man outside, and Evie knew that fine line had been stretched to near invisibility.

"I'll never go back," she whispered against the curtains. "Ever. I can't, I just can't." Her heart pounded so hard she wondered if she would die of a stroke before anyone knew where she was.

She slumped on the end of her bed; her gaze fixed on the wall opposite. She needed to concentrate and make a plan, but thoughts were hard to manage when she could hardly breathe for fear.

Calm yourself, Evie, she told herself. Calm. She thought of white fluffy clouds drifting across a deep blue sky and lost herself in the patterns of those imagined and half-remembered clouds. Breathe deep and slow, she repeated, until her thoughts and her heart slowed.

Only then did she ask herself the first question she needed to ask: How the hell had they found her? She'd been so careful, or so she believed, but obviously not careful enough. She examined all of her memories of the last few days. Every moment ran through her mind in slow motion, and finally she remembered where she had seen him.

Yesterday. At the market. Between the fish mongers and the butcher. She hadn't seen his face, but she recalled the jacket and the slouch. He'd almost run into her between the bread stall and the patisserie, but she'd thought nothing of it at the time. There were always a lot of people at the market.

She had seen him one last time as she'd drawn out of the market. He'd been surrounded by a bunch of street kids, and she had paid him little attention as she'd walked by on the opposite side of the street.

Had she made a mistake with how she had presented herself? She thought through that, too. Evie had kept her head covered with an old and oversized bonnet that helped shade her face and covered her hair. She'd worn a coat so large and without shape it had made her physique appear much larger. At least, that's what she'd thought.

She wondered, then, if his being there was a coincidence or not. She glanced through the window again and stared at him as he leaned against the wall.

A coincidence? No such thing. He looked as though he had nothing better to do, yet now that she watched with care, this man stared into the face of everyone who walked by. That spot had not been chosen on a whim.

Evie took a deep breath. Her time here had drawn to a close. If she stayed, she would never be safe again. Even if she left, there were no guarantees, but better to run with hope than to stay and be caught.

She drew the drapes partway across the window, and her room filled with shadows. In the darkest corner, between the edge of the bed and the washstand, she curled up with her knees pressed against her chest. If she made herself small enough, she might merge with the shadows and become invisible. If they couldn't see her, they couldn't find her, and perhaps they might forget that she existed.

She knew Bethwood and his men would never forget, though, and she pushed herself as hard as she could into the dark corner. Her eyes peered into every shadow, as though she expected Godwyn Bethwood to walk through the wall and grab her where she sat.

Evie pressed her face against her knees and closed her eyes. Without sight, the blackness offered some comfort. Her mind churned away, but after a while, after no one came to fetch her, her thoughts settled. Even her heart rate slowed so that it no longer pounded loudly enough to echo inside her ears.

In the background, she heard the deep and perpetual tick of the grandfather clock in the hallway downstairs. A peaceful sound, yet the never-ending tick and tock reminded her that time moved on, and that, for her, it had run out.

She rose to her feet, took several deep breaths, and ground her teeth together. She didn't have time to feel sorry for herself. She was tired of feeling like a criminal. She was tired of being scared, forced into hiding. She had done nothing wrong. Other than being born what she was. She was tired of being hunted and treated like an animal. But that's what she was, and she'd never be anything other than prey to them. A specimen, property, to be chased, collected, and locked away.

She had to do something.

She had to get away.

She would miss this lovely house, of course, and she would miss Mrs Hickman, her landlady, most of all. She smiled at the thought of Mrs Hickman. A small beacon in her darkness. Evie still remembered when she'd been invited to tea the first time. They'd sat in the parlour and talked. Most of their subject had been inconsequential:, local gossip, the state of the world, and, of course, the weather. They'd talked of the engineer, Iskabard Speare, and his new propellers that were the talk of the town. Most of all, Evie recalled that Mrs Hickman had made her feel like a normal human being.

As if on cue, she heard the shuffling steps of her landlady on the stairs down the hallway. She opened the door and saw the old woman on the landing.

"Mrs Hickman, what are you doing going up these stairs?" Evie asked. She rushed across the hall and offered Mrs Hickman her hand. "You shouldn't be climbing those steps. You know it makes your knees ache."

Mrs Hickman waved her off.

"I can manage, but I forget about my old bones," she said. "Think I should get one of those wireless things, or bell pulls so I can invite you to tea without having to face these steps."

"If it saved your knees, you could shout from the bottom of the stairs."

Ms Hickman shook her head. "Shout, indeed."

Evie smiled. "Perhaps not."

"Never mind. I knew you were in, Evie dear, and wondered if you would fancy a cup of tea with me?"

"Of course. How could I resist?" In her heart, though, she wanted to think of a way to escape. But she didn't want to be rude, not to Mrs Hickman. Besides, where was she going to rush off to?

"You can't resist, of course. And how would you fancy a slice of bread pudding with that tea? Old Vera at number thirty-two has made one of her large puddings and, bless her, gave me a good quarter of it. The moment I saw it, I thought of you. You need feeding up, and I never eat her puddings all myself. Better to share it than throw it away as waste." She shook her head. "Wasting food is a crime, and I'll have none of it in my house."

"A cup of tea and a slice of pudding would be wonderful, thank you for thinking of me," Evie replied.

"How could I not? A good stiff breeze would blow you over, and I would be remiss as a human if I did not consider your well-being."

"You have been so kind to me since I arrived. I know I've only been here a short while, but you have made me most welcome. Thank you."

Mrs Hickman waved her hands about as though she thought the compliment to be irrelevant, but she smiled and her eyes looked bright. "It's nothing more than any decent person would do," she said.

"I've been blessed, then, with the good fortune to stay with such a decent person."

"I would say we are both blessed."

"You'll never know how much." Evie didn't say any more, but she would never be able to forget this woman's kindness. Or her civility, and the grace with which she had made Evie feel like a human being. "I really do appreciate your kindness, and of course, your friendship. Most of all, I like those cups of tea in front of the fire."

"Get on with you, Evie Chester, it is the very least anyone can do. Besides, you've been very good company these last few days. I don't get many visitors, so maybe I should thank you."

"You're too kind," she said again. "I'll always cherish these moments."

Mrs Hickman gazed into Evie's eyes and rested her hand on her shoulder. "You're thanking me as though this is the last time we'll get to enjoy each other's company. You're going to run, aren't you, Evie?"

Evie averted her eyes and stared at one of the brass buttons on Mrs Hickman's short jacket. She always dressed well, as though she had someplace important to be. "Again?" she asked.

"You don't need to say anything, but I understand," Mrs. Hickman said. She stepped closer and whispered, "Are you Gifted, Evie?"

"Mrs Hickman? What are you suggesting?"

"Listen, Evie, you are not the first of your kind to be lodged here with me. I should have mentioned it earlier, and perhaps it would have put you at ease a little sooner. But you were near set to flight as soon as you arrived, and I didn't want to scare you off. I think you needed a stable place more than you needed me to understand your life."

Evie nodded.

"The Order often sends me their Gifted boys and girls."

"I'm not a child, Mrs Hickman, even if the Order did send me."

Mrs Hickman stared at Evie with eyes that were sharp despite her age. "A young woman, then, but to me you're all children no matter how old you are."

Evie looked at the floor. "Of course."

"Which means you are Gifted, aren't you?"

"Gifted? More like cursed. I'm a freak of nature, and I can never forget it."

"Evie," she said, and took hold of Evie's hand. "That's nonsense. Twelve Gifted girls have passed through my doors, and not one of them would I call freaks. Neither are you. Come on downstairs. Let us talk of this in the privacy of my rooms. If nothing else, we can make plans for your future. And if you must run, we must get you to a safe place."

Evie resisted the pull of her hand. "You don't understand

what you're doing. You mustn't be involved, Mrs Hickman. They might not treat you well if they found out."

Mrs Hickman snorted. "I know exactly what I'm doing. The Order placed you here. Do you think they would do that if they thought you were at risk from me?" She shook her head. "Your rent has been paid until the end of the month, and a line of credit exists if you wish to stay longer. As I see you now, I doubt you will stay that long, will you?"

Evie shook her head. "I don't know…"

"There's no need to fear me or this house. Of all the places in Bristelle, other than an Order-controlled house or ship, this is as safe as any place. If you need work, we can find you something to pay your way. Whatever you need, let me help."

"It's not safe, no place is safe," Evie repeated. "They'll find me."

"Let's talk about it, then. You can tell me who 'they' are, and why you are so worried all of a sudden," she said.

Mrs Hickman led the way down the stairs, along the hallway, and into the kitchen rather than the parlour. "Sit yourself down." She pointed to a narrow wooden chair in front of the cast iron range oven. Evie obediently sat where shown.

She served up two big cups of strong tea and added sugar to take away the stewed flavour. She sliced bread, slathered it with creamy butter, and topped it with lots of jam. She put it on a small white plate and handed it to Evie.

"Now that's a sarnie. I've not seen one like it since I was a kid, when…" Evie's voice faded away into memory.

"Well, dear, now you have had one of mine, and that can fill more recent memories, can't it? I can make many more of them if you like."

"Thank you."

"Now, Evie, I think you and I need to talk."

3

_____

E vie stared at the oven as Mrs Hickman settled herself in her chair. Almost in unison, they sipped hot tea and, as one, they clinked cup against saucer as they finished.

"Right then, now we are here, you best tell me everything," Mrs Hickman urged. "Let's see how I can help."

After a lifetime of abuse and other unpleasantness, this was only the second time in Evie's life that someone she barely knew had offered to help. She brushed away the unpleasant and unfamiliar sensation around her eyes. Emotion threatened to overwhelm her, but no tears fell. As far as she could recall, she had lost that ability. Still, strange how the eyes managed to hurt even without the tears.

"Someone is hunting you, aren't they, Evie? Do they think you are lost or something?"

"Yes…No…Not quite." She wasn't at all sure what she should say. Mrs Hickman was no innocent in the ways of the world, but to tell her would be to impose on her good nature. Did she want to? She had been nice, friendly, helpful, and although Evie liked her, she still had one question that remained unanswered: Could she be trusted?

At that, an image of two women came to her mind. She

saw the two women of the Order who had helped her escape. Magda and Ascara. She trusted them. They had led her here, to this house. They wouldn't have done so if they didn't have some trust in Mrs Hickman.

"Yes, Mrs Hickman, I'm not lost, I'm hunted, and I do not wish to be found."

"Tell me, Evie, what you have done to have so many people searching for you."

Evie thought of her answer and froze. "You said 'so many people.' Do you know something?"

"I have eyes to see, and I see a great deal. I'm old, too, and I have lived in these parts all my life. I know who is who and what is what."

"You don't know everyone."

"Well, dear, long before you were born, Mr Hickman and I ran the pharmacy and apothecary over on what was Millar Street. There is not a family I didn't meet when we ran the store, and in the same way that we'd diagnose and remember details about who had what, I can still remember the people who lived in this house." She shook her head. "Anyway, no matter what you say, I don't think it is all to do with your gifts, whatever they are."

"Mrs Hickman—"

"Eat your sandwich," Mrs Hickman interrupted. She didn't speak until Evie started to eat again. "As I said before, you are not the first young woman to come through my doors, and you will probably not be the last. I wanted to talk to you sooner, but I didn't want to interfere."

Evie took another bite of her sandwich, chewed, and swallowed.

Mrs Hickman picked up her cup of tea and stared into its depths. "It takes a while to build up trust, and you have not been here long enough to trust me."

"Mrs Hickman—"

"Well, never mind that. Let me tell you what I see, and what I see is men on the streets," Mrs Hickman said.

"There are always men on the streets," Evie countered.

"This is different. These men are more organised. More determined."

"Oh," Evie said. Her thoughts raced in circles as she tried to put this together into something useable.

"And these men? They were Bethwood's men, and the street kids flocked to them for a penny of attention. They were hunting for something, or someone."

Evie froze, her sandwich halfway between plate and mouth. "How do you know?" she asked, in little more than a whisper.

Mrs Hickman stared at her. "You can't live in Ardmore without grasping the nature of power and influence on the streets. Never underestimate the quiet women who people pass without a second thought. They are the ones who see all and speak nothing to anyone. And I can tell you, Vera gives away her puddings and takes away more news than you'll ever find in the Bristelle Times newspaper."

Mrs Hickman rose to her feet and shuffled over to the shelves in the corner of the room. She unwrapped a large chunk of bread pudding and cut two slices. A thin one she placed on a plate for herself, and the other, much thicker, she gave to Evie.

"Finish your sandwich and eat this," she said.

"Thank you."

"I made it my business, then, to listen a little more closely to what people said when I went out. The word is that they seek a small blonde woman with bright blue eyes. 'Frail looking,' they said, and that sounds quite a bit like you. Funny accent, they said."

There was no point in denying it anymore. "Yes, they're searching for me. I thought he might have forgotten."

"Bethwood? If you owe him a penny, he'll make sure you pay ten times as much for the cheek of owing him."

"Too right."

"I'm right, then, that the man who is hunting you would be Godwyn Bethwood?"

Evie nodded.

Mrs Hickman leaned over and patted Evie's hand. "Eat, dear. Nothing is going to happen here. Not today. Not any day, if I have my way."

Evie stared at her bread pudding. It looked so soft, and she could see the dried fruits inside. She tore off a small chunk and popped it into her mouth. It was all she'd imagined, full of fruity sweetness. It was lovely.

"Nice?" Mrs Hickman asked. "Vera makes a lovely pudding. She should sell it. She'd make a fortune."

"It's truly a dream, Mrs Hickman, thank you," Evie said.

Mrs Hickman nodded, satisfied with her answer. "You should call me Agatha. I think we are friends enough now, don't you think?"

"Yes," Evie agreed.

"Here we are, then. As I said, I don't understand what your Gift is, and I have no need to understand anything about it, either. That is your business, and your business only."

Evie finished eating her pudding. "Agatha, you are right in all things. Bethwood owns me as he would a slave, and the Order helped me escape."

"Slavery is illegal in all of the Angles, Evie. That's a well-known fact."

"It might be a fact, but that doesn't make it true out in the real world, especially if you're a Gifted one," Evie countered. "And people like Godwyn Bethwood don't give a hoot about the law."

"They can't do that. It's not right. Some laws cannot be broken, even by the likes of him."

"They can, and they do. In some parts of the world, it is an unforgiveable sin to be Gifted. Even here in the Angles, there are places, like the city and docks of Bristelle, where the rules are different. And if they can't own me, they must kill me and people like me."

Agatha stared at Evie's hands and neck. "Slaves are marked with the symbols of ownership. Where are your marks, Evie? I can't see them."

Evie returned the plate to the table and held out her hands. "My first owner used a cattle brand to put his mark on the back of my hand." She stopped for a moment when Agatha winced. "The second owner branded my neck with a number. The third, well, that would be Godwyn Bethwood, wasn't satisfied with one attempt. First, he tried to have me branded, and when that didn't work, he had me tattooed with his name. When that didn't work either, he tattooed and branded me with needles made bright from the heat of the furnace." Evie pulled back the collar of her blouse to show a neck unmarked by burn or ink. "Nothing took."

Agatha looked horrified. "That must have been—"

"Painful?" Evie finished for her.

Agatha nodded.

"It was. I've had the three owners. Not all of them have been careful with their property."

"I'm sorry, Evie."

"Sorry? Why would you be sorry? You did not do this."

"Sorry that you have had such pain and sorrow. It is not right."

Evie stared at the floor. "My life, since my gift manifested itself, has become measured in moments of survival. No one cares—"

"I care."

Evie looked into Agatha's eyes and believed her words. "That makes you one of very few people on this good earth."

Agatha rose to her feet. She took Evie's plate and added another slice of the pudding. "Eat," she said.

Eat? Evie thought she would burst with all she had eaten. A sandwich and two pieces of pudding, that was almost a week's worth of food. "I can't squeeze any more in me."

"Try harder and let me think."

Evie nibbled at the pudding. The silence between them was not an uncomfortable one, and she felt quite at ease considering she needed to work out what to do next.

"If you are a Bethwood slave, that would mean it's probably about money or power. Bethwood is not a stupid man, and he will cut his losses. To find one person with pennies for the streets is not a cheap thing. I'm not sure any Gift is worth the money he would have to spend to find you." She filled her cup with tea and returned to her seat. "It occurs to me that they are either scared of you, Evie, or—"

"Scared of me?" Evie interrupted. She stood up and drew her shoulders back to make the most of her full height, all five feet and possibly half an inch of it. "Does it seem as though those burly thugs should be scared of me? Until a few weeks ago, my home was a mattress in an old stable, where I was chained to a wall along with three other Gifted women. They are scared of me?"

Agatha looked horrified. "You were chained? In an outbuilding?"

Evie shrugged. "Well, it was better than the shed."

"If they are not scared of your physical presence, they must be scared of what you might do to them. With your gifts. Is your gift that valuable to them?"

Evie sat back in her seat. "I can't read minds or tell the future. I can't read auras, speak with the dead, or see off to faraway places. I can't predict the weather or sense the location of ores. I can't control fire, make wind, or part water. I can't hurt anyone with a touch or a look, either."

"So what do they want you for?"

Evie stared into the flames as they danced inside the oven.

Agatha had left the door open, and she saw the fire licking over wood and coal. "They think I'm a healer."

"Great goddess, no wonder they want you. A healer is a rare gift, and they would make a small fortune out of any healer they controlled."

"Yes, and they lost me."

"Now I see it," Agatha said. "You're a useful commodity, with great value, and you escaped. You ran from them. It isn't about the cost of you, but something more important. Ego. Money and ego is not a good combination. Always remember that, Evie."

"But I'm not a healer, though. They just think I am."

Agatha frowned. "I don't see how they could have mistaken what you do."

Evie had not planned to talk this much, but now that she had started to speak, she couldn't stop. "I don't heal at all, Agatha. I absorb sickness and the corruption of the body. I am like a cloth dipped in water. A sponge. Nothing more than a simple sponge."

"And that is the fullness of your skill?"

"What? What do you mean? Of course it is. We only get one skill."

"Most of the Gifted that I have met have some minor ability that is secondary to their main skill. Are you fully tested?"

"I don't have a secondary skill. Just the sponging."

"Listen to me, Evie. Gifts are never easy to understand, and they are not always as they seem. You need help to do this."

"I... I don't know…"

"Trust me, you cannot do this alone."

"Trust," Evie said, "is a very rare commodity."

"True enough, but that doesn't mean it can't be found."

Evie shook her head. She stared at Agatha. "How can it be so easy to find, when those you trust most in the world are the first ones to betray you? My mother and my father should have been the two people I could trust in times of trouble, instead they sold me."

Agatha flinched. "They were not good people, and you deserve better. First, we need to find you a safe place. A home where you are not held rigid with fear."

"I understand."

"Will you join the Order?" Agatha asked.

Evie shook her head.

"Why not, Evie? You would be safer with them. I could get the Order here to help you get away."

"I can't," Evie whispered. "It would be like being owned again. Like replacing one owner with another."

Agatha nodded as though she understood, but Evie didn't think anyone, least of all someone as respectable as Agatha Hickman, had the slightest idea of what it was like out there.

"It's too dangerous to run away all the time. The hunters get mad when they catch up with their prey," Agatha said.

"Probably best that I don't get caught, then."

"You can't spend your life running like you are some sort of criminal."

"What am I supposed to do, Agatha? Sit and wait for them to find me?"

"If you won't join the Order, you should go to the Towers in Knaresville. There are several there. There might be one in the North Angle highlands, but I am not sure about that. Either way, they will offer you safety and training."

"Towers? I have heard of the Towers," Evie said. "It is said, even in the pens of the slaves, that the Towers are the mark of the covenant between the great spirit of our Mother and the people."

"Yes, and Mother Earth herself protects those who embrace the power of her covenant," Agatha said.

"I couldn't see the powerful witches of the Towers being

interested in anyone like me," she said. No one wanted her here, why would anyone want her in a Tower either?

"Of course they would," Agatha said.

"I'm not sure a Tower is where I belong," she said.

"Either join the Order so they can see your Gift, or get yourself to something like the Tower of the Healers. These are the most sensible options. They will not only give you sanctuary, but they will also test the limits of your skill and teach you all you need to get by in this world."

Evie shook her head.

"The first step is to decide what it is that you want, Evie."

"I don't know. I don't want to be found. I don't want to be a slave or owned by anyone. I want a life like everyone else, I suppose."

"I understand that."

"It doesn't matter really, I can't stay here. They're too close to finding me," she said. "To them, I am worth less than the muck under the bottom of a shoe—"

"No, Evie!"

She shrugged. "But the choice between the Towers of Knaresville or the Order doesn't sound like much of a choice."

"You don't have to choose anything yet. We can make plans for your getaway, and we'll try and keep your options open."

"Thank you," Evie replied. "I'm really grateful for all of your help and kindness."

Agatha smiled. "Crossing Bethwood is not a good thing to do, but he is a bully, and we should not let bullies ruin our lives. We need to be practical about things." She stroked her chin. "First, we need to dull that hair of yours. Long blonde hair stands out. I can't do anything about your eyes, and you'll have to concentrate on losing your accent."

Evie snorted. "The last time I tried to hide my accent, they thought I was slow-witted."

"Does it matter?"

She shrugged. "I suppose not."

Agatha busied herself making another pot of tea. She used a lot of tea leaves, though, and only a touch of water.

"That looks like it will be a bit strong to drink."

"It's not for drinking," she replied. "I'm going to see if the tea will dull and stain your hair a bit." She muttered to herself, "Once upon a time, I would have been able to make a dye that would turn your hair black, but I don't have such things here, and I have no time to brew something. I'd need walnuts, too, and I don't have any." She shook her head. "Tea will have to do."

"I've never heard of such things." Evie paused in thought. "Will it work?"

"No idea, but if it stains the pot, it should do the same to your hair. At the very least, it will dull it and make you less obvious. It would work much better if we repeated the process over several days, but I am not sure you'll allow such a length of time?"

Evie shook her head.

"I can't do anything about your eyes, mind."

"If it doesn't work, cut my hair off and tuck it under a bonnet."

"If it comes to that, we will. Shame to cut your hair if we don't have to." She looked at Evie. "If we cut it, I could try and make you appear like a boy."

Evie pointed at her chest. "These might give me away."

Agatha nodded. "You're probably right."

4

———————

The days passed in fear, but it was better to be hidden than caught. But how long could she hide away whilst she wondered about her future?

Her life became split between two locations: her room and Agatha's kitchen. Her visits to the kitchen were not just social calls, but practical events. Several times a day, Agatha would soak her hair in strong tea and use a leather tie to keep her wet tresses out of the way. They repeated the process so often that Evie wondered if her hair would ever be dry.

Today, she underwent the process for the last time. Her life was about to change. Again.

She examined all the items she and Agatha had collected as useful and shook her head. They'd put aside a heavy skirt several sizes too big. She had a several layers of petticoats to add bulk, and they'd made a pile of small sleeve puffs that they planned to use to alter her shape to something rather more rotund.

Evie thought about the two layers of shirts, the woollen cardigan, and the extra thick and lumpy overcoat that would hide her. "I think I'll melt in all these clothes."

"It will help hide who you are. They won't be looking for a thicker woman."

Evie picked up a pair of shoes that had been altered to give her a few extra inches in height. She turned them over and over. "I can't wear these."

"They are not as uncomfortable or as awkward as they seem," Agatha said.

"I'll break my neck if I try to walk. I couldn't run away, for a start."

"Yes, but if they don't recognise you, then you won't need to run anywhere."

"I'll take my chances with footwear I'm used to. I can't rely on any one thing to protect me."

Agatha nodded and reached for Evie's hair. "It's a pity the tea didn't do a better job. It's dulled it a little, but I'm not sure it's enough. Blonde is such a rare colour in Bristelle, and I don't want to ask anyone for advice in case it draws attention to us."

"Cut it, then," Evie said.

"But your beautiful hair!"

"My beautiful hair is going to get me killed. Either cut my hair or poke my eyes out. It's the two together that make me stand out."

"And your accent."

She cleared her throat, and when she spoke, she made her voice quieter, drew out the sounds, and slurred them together.

Agatha laughed. "Yes, you really do sound like you're slow-witted. At least they won't hear the accent because they'll not stop laughing at you."

"I'm happy if all they do is laugh."

That seemed to focus Agatha's thoughts. "Are you aware that men have started knocking on doors?"

"Have they? Why?"

"They are asking about a short woman with long blonde hair and blue eyes."

"That's me they are asking about, isn't it?"

Agatha nodded. "Old Vera called the guards on them, but that won't stop them for long."

"I know," Evie said, her voice quiet. "If I'm to leave, it will have to be today."

"Let's get you ready, then. Do you have your things?"

Evie placed her personal items in a small leather travel bag. She didn't have much, and everything she carried had been given to her by the Order.

Agatha wrapped the bag in an old sheet and several cloths and piled it all into a washer basket. There it was: her entire disguise as a washerwoman.

Agatha, however, was busy rummaging through a small box. "I have scissors in here someplace."

Ten minutes later, Agatha hacked at Evie's hair, cutting it off half an inch above her shoulders. "Your beautiful hair," she muttered. "You look like a boy. This is such a dreadful shame."

Evie thought that Agatha looked ready to cry, and she didn't want her upset anymore. She grabbed Agatha's hands. "Don't worry about me or my hair. It's all…" she started to say. Instead of words, her mind filled with the sense of infection in Agatha's bones. The marks of her age for the most part, but those signs of age were sore and inflamed. Soon, Agatha would be unable to do much. Her fingers would curl and lock in a painful rictus. Her back, already curled with age, would seize up, and the inflammation would spread unchecked.

"You hurt," Evie said.

"What?"

"You must be in dreadful pain."

"Evie?"

Without another thought, Evie's skill and gift rose up, and

like the sponge she was, she soaked up all the infections locked within Agatha's frail body. She knew, because age was no disease to be cured so easily, that she couldn't heal Agatha, but she could help relieve the burning in her old joints. After all she'd done, it was the least that Evie could do.

"What was that, Evie? What did you do? I feel different."

Evie stared at the floor. "Is that good or bad?"

"Very good. I feel fantastic!"

"That is my gift to you. Your knees should feel far better, for a while at least."

Agatha stared at her. "That is how your gift works? You heal by taking away the pain?"

Evie shrugged. "Something like that, yes."

Agatha drew her into a tight embrace. "Whatever happens, Evie, live and never give up. Find yourself a safe place. The good you can do is too much a gift to lose it." She smiled. "Too good to waste on the likes of Bethwood and his cronies."

"I will," Evie replied. Then, for the first time in many years, she wrapped her arms around another person and embraced Agatha back. "And you must look after yourself, too, Agatha Hickman. I will come and visit you when it is safe."

"Good. You do that." Agatha stepped backwards and wiped her eyes on a small cotton cloth. "Now, before I cry and make little sense, I have one more gift."

"Agatha—"

She held up a hand to stop Evie from talking. "No, let me give you this." She handed Evie a rail ticket and a letter. "The letter is from the Order. Remember the two women who escorted you here?"

"Magda Stoner and Ascara?" Evie asked.

Agatha nodded. "Yes, I think so. They asked that you read this once you're on your way."

"Agatha, I can't read."

"Do you want me to read it to you?"

Evie considered that for a moment. "No. Thank you."

"Why not?"

"I want to be able to find a place for myself before I know what she says. Magda wants me to join the Order, and I'm not sure that's what I want."

"Fair enough. You must decide these things for yourself."

"I will, but thank you." Evie turned away for a moment. She didn't know why she didn't want anyone to read her letter. It seemed as though it was hers and hers alone. If anyone read it, it was no longer just hers, and she had so little of her own that she wanted to savour it a little longer.

"If you can get to the Towers, any one of the women there can read it," Agatha said "I think of all the Towers I am aware of, you should go to either the Healers' or the Rainbow Tower."

"Rainbow or Healers'. Got it."

"Or find an Order representative."

"Order or Towers," Evie repeated.

Agatha nodded. "In the last few days, I have thought about nothing other than how to get you out of here, and out of Bristelle. I've got it all planned, Evie, and this is what you must do." She took a seat next to the fire. "You need to catch the post train from Bristelle North Street Station at five-oh-five precisely. It is the evening postal service, and it's scheduled to stop at every single station on its route around the west coast of Mid-Angle. Because they're transferring the mail, there might be a wait be a wait at the platform. Stay on the train, though, until you reach Knaresville. Don't stay there too long, as it leaves the city an hour before dawn and travels straight back to Bristelle."

"I understand."

"Good. Please be careful, Evie."

"I will. But I'm not at all sure about the disguise."

"Nonsense, you look grand." Agatha pulled Evie this way

and that, turned her round and round, and prodded and pulled until Evie thought she was some errant child being punished.

"Steady," Evie said.

Agatha clicked her tongue and pulled at Evie's skirt and blouse until it hung out one side. She readjusted the skirt so it hung from Evie's waist at a less than pleasing angle.

"There. Now you're a fine washerwoman after a long day. I hardly recognise you."

"It's as good as it can get, I suppose."

"Good enough, I hope. Now, do you remember what you have to do?"

"Yes."

"Let's go over it again, because it can be complicated. You go through the back gate, into the Ardmore Ginnels—"

"The what?" Evie interrupted.

"The alleys at the back. That's what they call them here, ginnels. Beware the ones to the southern end, they're shorter and wider, more like lanes than alleys."

"All right, I got that, but last night you called them the alleys. Sorry to interrupt."

Agatha nodded. "Turn right into the alleyway, second left to the end, left again, follow the ginnel to the end right into Askin's Lane. At Askin's, you should merge in with the other women on their way back from the washrooms. Follow the way to Esperet Road and turn into the lanes there. There's a large rhododendron. Hide the basket behind it and backtrack to the main street. Don't worry about the basket, I'll get it later."

"I've got that."

"Be safe, Evie. Be safe."

"As a locked house."

Evie hoisted the wash basket onto her shoulder and headed out the back door. She adjusted the weight of the basket as she crossed the yard to the back gate.

"Hang on," Agatha said. She unlocked and opened the gate and looked outside. She nodded. "On you go."

"Thank you," Evie said.

"May the Mother of us all watch over you," Agatha said.

Evie slipped into the lanes, and the gate closed behind her. She was on her own now.

She glanced left and right. The alley stretched away from her in both directions. Three feet wide, the sides stood high above her head, but the materials used to maintain this height varied from house to house. Fences, sheet metal, and walls. At regular intervals, gates allowed access to the backyards of each house.

Evie's heart pounded against her ribs. She wanted to knock on the gate and ask Agatha to hide her a little bit longer. Too late for that, though. She had to move on. She also knew that if she didn't move soon, she would be noticed, and she didn't want or need that kind of attention. She peered along the alley once more, and set off.

Into the labyrinth she strode, with purpose and determination. She could do this. Every step took her further away from trouble and closer to freedom. Free.

She'd not gone far when she saw a small child racing down the alley in her direction. Scruffy, small, and dirty. He saw her, came to a halt, stared at her, and raced off back the way he'd come.

Odd, she thought, but ignored it. After all, everyone used these alleys. The kids obviously used it as a thoroughfare off the main streets. Maybe he didn't want to be caught scrambling over the fences. The kids did that sometimes, to see what they might be able to pinch.

In the distance, she heard the sounds of the city. The alleys seemed to muffle the noise, and now that she heard whistles and a low hum, she knew she had almost reached the roads. The crash of the dockers loading and unloading echoed even in the narrow confines of the alleys. But the sounds of the river were never far away.

Her progress set her heart pounding again. She was almost at Askin's Lane and ready to merge with normal people to hide in plain sight. Her stomach churned. "Evie Chester," she told herself, "get a grip. Nearly there."

Onwards. She marched along as though driven. After all, she had a place to be and a time in which to do it.

It was all going so well. She was safe.

And then she wasn't.

There were two of men blocking the next exit. Both of them were well built, with broad shoulders. They wore brown trousers, loose jackets, and the heavy boots of the workman, not the shoes of the gent.

They slouched against the walls and spread themselves until they blocked the alley. One, the taller of the two, had a dagger in his hand and was cleaning his fingernails with it.

She slowed her step and wondered if they were here for a reason. Nothing better to do? Waiting for anyone who might come this way? Or for someone in particular, like her?

She didn't think they were here for her. How could they be? No one knew she would be here. How could they? Besides, she didn't even look like herself.

Her thoughts dashed to her landlady. She wouldn't, would she? She dismissed the thought as unworthy. Agatha Hickman had been so kind and thoughtful.

Right then, Evie decided the how of it didn't matter. What was important was that they were here, and she didn't want to meet them. Just in case. She backed away, slowly. Back down the alleyway. She didn't even pay attention to where she stepped. She didn't need to, not when she had walked this way not five minutes before. She moved with some care, but more than anything she needed to put space between her and them.

Then she stopped.

Something hard and sharp enough to be felt through all of her layers of clothing pressed into her back.

"No way out. Not this way, darlin'," said a rough voice behind her.

Evie manoeuvred herself against one wall and peered over one shoulder to the man behind. Well, bugger. There were two more of them. Dark haired, swarthy complexion, and dark eyes. These men had no jackets, but they wore dirty waistcoats with brass buttons. They both carried short, crude, cudgels in one hand, and belt daggers in the other. Short or long, a blade or a cudgel would hurt.

The ones who had been in front of her sauntered down the alleyway to join their intimate little group. Evie had nowhere to run and climbing the fence or the walls was not really going to help.

"What you doing?" she asked. She tried her slow voice, the one that hid her accent.

"Thought she were foreign?" asked one of the guys in a waistcoat.

"I think you must be looking for someone else," Evie said.

One of the chaps in jackets eyed her thoughtfully. He smiled, and his teeth, all crooked and black, made him look as though he'd chomped on a chalkboard. "I don't think so, Evie," he said. He spoke with the right amount of disdain for Evie to know that she was in trouble and no mistake. Either he was a Bethwood boy or an anti-Gifted thug.

When he smiled at her, she knew for sure. "Mr Bethwood would like a word with you," he said with a smirk.

"Bethwood says you owe him," said the shorter man at his side. "Now come along quiet like, and we'll not have to do you any harm, witch."

"I owe no one anything. I think you have me confused with another. I do the washing is all," she said. She sniffed the air. The shortest one, the one without a jacket, was sick. Sick enough to reek of badness. Why should she care? She didn't know him.

Black Teeth snorted. "Yeah, right. Well, you're worth a right nice sum. If you're the wrong 'un, he can sort it out. Myself? It's good money, and ya don't say no to money nor Bethwood. Got it?"

"You'll stink in hell for this," Evie said.

Two of them snickered. "Feisty one, too."

Black Teeth's face grew stern. "Shut your fucking 'ole," he said. He clenched his fist, and as he drew back, Evie tried to step out of the way. It wasn't far enough. He punched her so hard, she didn't even have time to think about how much it hurt before the blackness came. She remembered no more.

E vie woke up to find herself in a darkened room, laid out on a narrow bed. A thin layer of material lay between herself and the springs of the bedstead, but that didn't stop the metal from grinding into her back when she moved.

Her hands bore the weight of the tight manacles around her wrists. When she moved, she heard the slithering clank of chains as they ran along the metal bedstead. She yanked on the chains, even swivelled around on the bed to use her feet for leverage, but they did not give. With every failed attempt, Evie found herself becoming increasingly frantic. No matter what she did, she couldn't pull free.

Caught.

Focus, Evie. Focus. Take deep breaths. Deep breaths.

"Focus," she said aloud.

She rubbed her jaw where she had been punched. It hurt, and her head throbbed. The noise of the chains did not help, but she couldn't simply lie there and do nothing.

She took a few deep breaths until the panic wore off. The calmer she became, the deeper her breaths grew and the more control she regained. She looked around and focussed her attention on her surroundings.

She lay on a bed. A bed in a room, so she hadn't been placed in the pens. Darkness dominated, but a little lamplight crept in from under the door, and she managed to see at least some of the basic details.

At a rough guess, she thought the room to be a good twelve or thirteen feet square. It had only one door, which she assumed would be locked. No way out of here unless the guards grew lax. They did, sometimes; especially when the prisoner was shackled. She hoped she were so lucky.

Opposite to the door, she could see the outline of a window shutter, and the weak glow that seeped around the wooden frame. It would be soon be dark outside, she surmised, so she hadn't been knocked out for too long.

The bed was of a standard iron-framed construction. Metal and leather strapping under the metal springs gave the bed support but no easy means of escape.

The wall next to the bed appeared plain and unbroken and, without better light, didn't promise much help. Evie sat up and pressed her back against the wall, at least she needn't be worried about being attacked from behind.

At the side of the bed stood a small table, upon which she saw the outline of a small jug and washbowl. Neither looked useful at the moment. She saw an armchair in the corner, and for now she deemed it an unnecessary item and ignored it as well.

Instead, her attention focussed on the metal bands that encircled her wrists. They were so tight that the metal chafed against her skin, and if she weren't careful, she'd do more harm than good. She couldn't wriggle out of them.

She turned her attention to the chains. They were a good set of links, and Evie knew well-made ironworks when she saw it. It would not be easy to escape either the manacles or the chains.

A sound caught her ear. In the darkness, a shape in the corner shifted and moved. She heard the click of a switch, and a small lamp added a feeble glow to the room. This house had electrics. This was no cheap house in the slums.

"Hello, Evie," said a man.

She recognised his voice. Godwyn Bethwood. "Bastard!" she cried out.

"It is lovely to see you, too. I'm so glad I found you again." He rose to his feet. He was a big man, close to six feet tall and almost as wide. She didn't think anyone could become the boss of a bunch of thugs if they were skinny or wimpish. The boss had to be someone they feared, and Bethwood was that kind of man.

He wore a good suit, well made and well fitted. His waistcoat looked most fancy, with fine stitchwork and bright colours and the buttons that seemed to glow in the half light. Out on the street, he would stand out as well-bred, a perfect gent.

Evie had only seen him up close once before, and he'd been wearing a blood-spattered leather apron. She had never asked him why it was so messy. Mostly she didn't want to know.

"There's no point struggling," he continued. "The chains are new forged and tested to ensure you don't escape me again."

He seemed to forget that chains had nothing to do with her last escape.

"In case you're wondering, I'll not hire you out to any more incompetent oiks who'll let you run away. I'm not losing you to stupidity again."

"I didn't run away. I was saved by people who care," she said.

"Is that right? Now look where you are."

"Let me go." Right then, Evie wished she had taken

Magda's offer to join their Order. Then she would have avoided this for sure.

"Come now, Evie, you know that's not possible. You cost me a pretty penny, and you have yet to earn your keep." He straightened his clothing so he looked perfect. "I have a great deal of work for you to do. Things have changed whilst you were absent, but I have reason to find out what it is you can do."

"Like a test?" she asked.

He didn't answer her question, but instead said, "Now, you either agree to do as you are told, without chains, or I use you as you are until you are as much use as a dirty rag." He took his pocket watch out and checked the time. "I will give you half of the hour to think about things."

Half an hour? What did that have to do with anything?

"Why?" she asked.

He snapped the watch case closed and slipped the timepiece back inside his pocket. "I have a dinner meeting with a few business associates. One is sick. I need you to heal him."

"How many?" Evie asked.

"Just one. Heal him, but no purging until you are in private."

"Why?"

"You ask too many damned fool questions, Chester. Do as you are told, and I won't have to give you any punishments. Understand?"

"I understand."

"Good." He sighed. "Listen, Chester, and listen well. I have a number of people, important people, and many of them require your services. We will line you up with people, fine ladies and gents. These are the people who can pay, and one day, maybe you will pay back what you cost me. I'll not waste you on petty people any more. You have my fullest attention and I'll select who you see. Let's see the fullest extent of your skills, shall we? Do what you do, no fuss and no mess."

"Sure," she said.

"You asked about purging, as you call it. Well, these are the sort of people who have no need, and no wish, to see the fruits of your gifts, understand?"

Evie understood. They made the shit and everyone else had to live in it. "And when will you let me go?"

"We will discuss that another time," he answered.

Evie glared at him with a degree of defiance she did not really feel. The net had closed around her, and she had been caught. There would be no second escape. Bethwood would make sure of it.

He put his foot on something on the floor and slid it towards Evie. The washing basket. Evie held her breath.

"Don't worry, it is all there," he said.

She stared at the basket as though she could see inside the linen and the bag inside.

"All there except the train ticket. I've sold that, and it will be deducted from the balance sheet of what you cost me. Less a commission for the costs of cashing it in."

"Bastard."

"Yes, you have mentioned such a thing already." He waved something in the air, and even in the dim light, Evie knew he had her letter. "Can you read, Evie Chester?"

She didn't answer.

"You can't, can you? Would you like me to read your letter for you?" He didn't wait for a response but pulled out a small pocket knife and sheared through the edge of the envelope. "Let's see what it says, shall we?"

"No, it's mine."

"What's yours is mine." He smiled. "Unless you agree to stop being such a nuisance and give me the respect I'm due. I'm tired of your ungrateful attitude. If it continues, I may well put you down like a diseased dog."

"Put me down, then. See if I care."

"You will care after I have chained you down and sold your body to every bug-ridden docker this side of the waters. I will recover my expenses, and your recovery has been an expense I did not wish to incur. I will be reimbursed." He laughed. "I own you, and everything you have is mine." He pulled out the letter and started to read.

There was nothing Evie could do.

After he had finished, he threw the letter on top of her things. "I tell you what, do as you are told, and I will have the letter read out to you." Bethwood pointed to the small bedside table. "There is water there. Clean yourself up and get ready to meet the client."

Evie didn't move. "I thought I had half an hour to think it through?"

Bethwood fiddled with his sleeve cuff. "You had. Now you need to clean yourself up. You've blood on your face, and the client would rather you were clean and unsullied, not as though you'd slept in the gutter."

"Right," she said.

"And if you should consider being awkward, think about this—if you fail me, or you do something to embarrass me, you will not see another sunrise. However, that last night will seem to last an eternity for you. Understood?"

Evie nodded.

"I'm sorry, what did you say?"

"I'm clear about the instructions."

"Good. Clean up, and I will send someone to fetch you shortly."

Just like that, Evie's future had been set.

5

Bethwood ushered Evie outside and into a small courtyard. Gas lamps adorned the walls and bathed the courtyard in a pale glow. At the centre of the courtyard stood a substantial barouche-style four-wheel carriage with black woodwork and gold-coloured trim. A collapsible calash roof lay fully open, and the seats inside were plush and comfortable.

The matched pair of black horses was so well kept, their coats shone. They stomped their feet and chomped at the bit, eager to be off. The driver and coachman wore matching livery and kept the horses in place.

Behind the coach, a man that Evie had never seen before leaned against the back wall. He wore a hat set low over his eyes so no one could determine where his gaze fell. He gave Evie the shivers.

"Ever been in a carriage of this sort?" Bethwood asked her.

She shook her head.

"Luxury like this is the sign of power and wealth. Enjoy it whilst you can," he said. He straightened his jacket and pulled at his cuffs.

Evie took a closer look at him. He dressed very smartly. His burgundy waistcoat not only had gems on the button detail, but the design had been sewn with gold thread. His shirt and collar were good, white cotton. From the outside, he appeared to be a very fine gent indeed. Nothing like Evie expected.

Who was Bethwood, she wondered. The fine gent here, or the bully he had been inside? The kind who wore a blood-spattered apron and did his own dirty work?

"Come, Evie, stop dawdling," Bethwood said.

As they approached, the coachman opened the door and lowered the step. He stood still, his gaze directed forward, as he waited for Bethwood to react.

The other man, the one who had leaned on the wall, tried to get into the coach with them, and Bethwood frowned. "Mr Grobber, you can ride at the back."

"That's for luggage," he replied in a rough voice.

"If you say so," Bethwood answered.

"Sir, my job is to take care of—"

"I am quite able to do that in my own carriage," Bethwood interrupted.

From the expression on Grobber's face, he was not pleased at the exclusion.

"Now, Evie, please sit. The ride is not too long." He gestured for her to climb inside. "I am glad you agreed to be reasonable. You look most respectable, all things considered. This bodes well for our future relationship."

Relationship? That would suggest a choice, and what choice did she have?

Evie straightened her plain woollen skirt. Even in an almost pristine cotton blouse, she dressed in simple form. Like a domestic. She knew that was where she would be placed, with the service staff. At least she wouldn't go around with a collar and chain. He'd left her some dignity. She wasn't sure Grobber would have.

After half an hour of clattering through the streets of Bristelle, the carriage pulled into the short driveway of a huge house. An ornate wall, topped with wrought iron fencing, surrounded the house and grounds. When Evie exited the carriage, she stood on the driveway and stared at the outside as though all thought eluded her.

"Come on, Evie, don't stare," Bethwood said.

At the front door, he waited until Grobber rang the bell for him. A minute later, the door creaked open.

A tall man, thinner than a dried-out bulrush, opened the door. Pale-skinned and dour, he sported a moustache so thin it looked painted.

"Mr Bethwood, good to see you again," the reedman said. "Mr Ellis-Wearing has left instructions that we must assist you in any way we can." He turned his attention to Evie and Grobber but didn't say anything to them. He pursed his lips as though they presented an affront to his position.

Bethwood put his hand on Evie's shoulder. "I think it best we go straight to the kitchens where this one can wait until required."

"Very well, sir. Let me show you the way. Best we go through the house at this time rather than the back way."

"As you wish," Bethwood said.

As soon as they entered the kitchen, Bethwood pushed Evie towards a stool in the corner. "Sit there and stay put until you're summoned. Do anything wrong, and there will be consequences." He ignored the cook, who stood behind the kitchen table and stared at them all.

"I understand," Evie said. She didn't mind. The kitchen was warm and bright, and the glorious aromas of roasting food made her stomach rumble. Evie would have been happy to sit amongst these aromas all day and all night if allowed.

"I'll leave Mr Grobber here to see that you are all right," he added.

Whether he stayed or left made no odds to Evie. She cast

her gaze to the floor and hunched down. With luck, no one would notice her.

"Excuse me, what is going on?" asked the cook.

"Nothing. Mind your business," Grobber said.

Evie glanced up.

The cook, a large woman by any standards, her cheeks all red and rosy, stood in the middle of the room, her legs apart and her hands on her hips. She held a large wooden spoon in one large fist, and it protruded forward like a sword.

Evie noted that no matter the robustness of her colour or her pose, the cook radiated a sense of folding in on herself, as though diminished in some way. Evie knew as she looked at her that the woman wasn't well.

"I said, what is going on?" the cook asked once more.

"And I said nothing," Grobber repeated.

The cook frowned and pulled back her shoulders. Fully upright, with her shoulders back, she was as tall as Grobber, and perhaps as tall as Bethwood himself.

She jabbed the wooden spoon in Grobber's direction. "You shut up. I will speak with the organ grinder, not the monkey."

The woman turned her attention to Bethwood. "And yes, I know you are a rich and important gent and you are very welcome upstairs, but this is the house of Mr Ellis-Wearing, and you have no say in this household, nor in the running of this kitchen. Understand?"

"Yes, ma'am," Bethwood said.

She turned back to Grobber. "You. If you have no use but to mind the girl, then stand outside the door. I don't care what you do outside—guard every window, the birds, and the flies on the compost for all I care. Right now, you will get the hell out of my kitchen."

Grobber turned his attention to Bethwood, but Bethwood turned and left without saying another word.

Evie grinned; she couldn't help it.

The cook glared at Grobber, and he did nothing but

grumble every step of the way out the kitchen door. Just to be sure, she slammed the door shut on him.

The cook wasn't finished. She turned her attention to Evie and stared.

Evie stared back, and in the meanest way, said, "I would get out of your kitchen if permitted, but if I did, it would not go well for me." Her stomach rumbled and gurgled.

"Are you hungry, child?" the cook asked.

Evie pulled back her shoulders. "I'm no child."

The cook nodded, as though the response explained everything. "My name is Mrs Arkwright, and I'm the cook here." She turned away and cut a thick slice of bread. She sliced some ham and put it on top. "You can call me Cook or Mrs Arkwright," she said.

"Yes, Cook."

"And what do they call you?"

"Evie," she answered.

"When was the last time you ate?" she asked.

Evie shrugged. "Yesterday?" She didn't sound so sure.

"Poor child," Mrs Arkwright said. She handed Evie the bread and ham. "Eat this. I'll have some hot food for you in a bit."

"Thank you," Evie said. She seemed to have this effect on women. First, they thought her a child, and then they wanted to feed her up. Evie could not understand such kindness, though, and from another stranger, too.

"Cup of tea?"

"I would love one," Evie replied. "Although you're too busy to make tea. Shall I make a cuppa for you?"

Mrs Arkwright smiled. "Thank you."

Evie jumped to her feet. Mrs Arkwright had asserted her rights in the kitchen, and that meant freedom of a kind. Evie wondered if she should try to escape, but she had no place to go and if found again, she had no illusions as to how bad it might get. Besides, Mrs Arkwright had been kind; she would not repay her trouble with the nastiness that Bethwood would create for her should Evie disappear.

She couldn't forget the fact that she'd escaped once, and her freedom hadn't lasted, not really. She would wait. Make plans and be better organised for next time.

Evie found her way around the iron range, boiled water, found the pot, and made the tea. It was nice to do it for herself for a change. It almost felt like freedom.

Mrs Arkwright gave her a once-over. "So, why are you here?" she asked. "You're not a tart, you ain't here for the cooking, and, well, you have a guard and Mr Bethwood." She paused for a moment. "He was not born to the wealth he displays. And I think his business is less than righteous. Still, he claws his way up through the social circles with greater success than most."

Evie wasn't sure what to say to that. She sat on her stool and tried not to draw attention to herself.

"Well, never you mind," Mrs Arkwright said. She turned her attention to the kitchen table and cleared things away. She stared at the clock for a few moments. "Pastry time, then. Let's hope the guests are not going to be delayed."

Mrs Arkwright wiped the tabletop and sprinkled flour over the rolling area. She uncovered the pastry and moved it to the centre of the table, dosed her rolling pin with flour, and started to work on the dough. She hummed as she worked, and for a moment, Evie found her thoughts transported back to a time she had all but forgotten.

She remembered, or possibly imagined, a time when she lived in a small village in the shade of the mountains. In her memories, or her dreams, her grandmother kneaded bread dough and sang to herself.

It took all her energy to shake off such thoughts. Looking backwards had no value except to remind her she no longer had a family. It underlined how awful her life had become. If such a life had existed, it had vanished in money exchanged and years of separation.

Her eyes started to prickle, but she wouldn't let herself cry. Not here. She turned to the Charles Brothers ironworks oven that had been built into the wall and glared so hard she did not hear or see Mrs Arkwright approach. With some surprise, she jumped when the woman rested her hand on her shoulder and took her hand with the other. Even worse than the shock of the woman's closeness was her touch. Skin to skin.

Sickness rolled into Evie in waves of darkness and hit her in the chest like a hammer blow. She couldn't breathe. She could hardly stand.

Mrs Arkwright stared. Her expression was a mixture of horror and concern. "What's the matter, dear?"

Evie jumped off her stool and separated herself from Mrs Arkwright before she absorbed too much of the sickness. She needed to regain distance, if only for a moment. She sucked at the air with the desperation of someone drowning. "You're unwell," she breathed.

"Yes, dear," she said. "I know." She frowned and took a step back as she realised what Evie had said. "You can tell?"

Evie turned away. She didn't want to see her face. She had seen enough disgust on enough faces to know that it was easier this way. Agatha had been an exception, but she had links with the Order, so her actions were no surprise. Here, though, it was different, and she expected a harsh word at the very least.

"Gifted?" Mrs Arkwright whispered.

Evie tried to make herself even smaller.

"You should put some sugar in that tea. No wonder you're so skinny. Well, that and being a part of Godwyn Bethwood's set."

"What?" Her reaction took Evie by surprise. So much so that she glanced up, expecting to see some form of hate or disgust, in spite of the words. What she saw instead was the same look that had graced her grandmother's face when she couldn't understand how Evie had got herself into one scrape or another. It was funny, she thought, how easy it was to slip back in time and see a past long gone. To see things she had so readily forgotten.

"Why are you here?" Mrs Arkwright asked.

"Aren't you repulsed by my presence?"

"Why would I be repulsed by someone who carries the blessing of our Mother?"

"I don't understand."

Mrs Arkwright smiled, and the warmth in her face made her eyes sparkle. "Once upon a time, the Gifted were revered, not reviled. And maybe one day they will be revered again."

Evie sat with her mouth open. "Not reviled?"

"Exactly. Never be ashamed of who you are, no matter what people tell you. You're blessed. Keep that thought next to your heart, and never let anyone tell you otherwise."

Mrs Arkwright patted Evie's cheek, then went back to her work. "Well, if you do things with sickness, I suppose that explains why you're here. Mr Ellis-Wearing has been a little under the weather of late. Perhaps you can make him feel more like himself."

"I don't know if I can until I see him."

Mrs Arkwright shook her head. "What I don't understand is what you are doing here with Bethwood."

"Because I am his, and it is better to be here than living in a slum doing goodness knows what."

"His?"

"Yes."

"I don't understand. Are you his daughter?"

Evie tried not to be horrified at the suggestion. She shook her head. "No. I'm his slave and there is no way out."

"There is always a way out, you just have to be ready when someone opens the door." She uncovered a fruit loaf on a stand. She cut a thick slice of the cake and handed it to Evie. "Eat."

Evie took the offered food and nibbled at the edges. Her stomach growled, and she resisted the urge to stuff as much as possible into her mouth all at once. "Do you want me to make you better?"

Mrs Arkwright shook her head. "If the Great Mother wills it, I am ready to meet the beyond when it is my time."

"Silly. I can make you better now," Evie said. She reached for her hand.

"You shouldn't," she said.

Yet Evie saw the pain in the cook's eyes. She knew the torture of sickness and approaching death, and although she would wish to live, she had already made peace with the inevitable. Mrs Arkwright gripped her hand that she almost crushed Evie's fingers. It was a reaction driven more from uncertainty than fear, Evie thought.

"You deserve to be well," Evie said. "I can make you feel better, at least for a while."

"I shouldn't impose," she repeated, but she didn't remove her hand from Evie's.

"The sickness is in your chest, and it is not too late to make a difference. Let me help you. Let me make your days easier."

Mrs Arkwright nodded. "All right."

Evie reached out and opened herself. The sickness came to Evie in bits, almost as though it had a mind of its own and didn't want to leave. No one wanted to leave a comfortable house, even when the house was crumbling and dying.

She fought against the slow crawl of the illness and called to it with every ounce of willpower. Like sludge, it came to her and swarmed into Evie's hand.

Lines of black wriggled under her skin and burrowed through her fingers. Evie almost cried out at the pain of it. Like hundreds of splinters writhing under her skin. The nails on Evie's hand turned yellow and green, and she concentrated, waiting for the moment they started to leak their poison. This was the worst part. Her fingers swelled and turned purple as the infection grew. She readied herself for the moment when her skin split open the infection escaped.

Mrs Arkwright broke the contact. "Stop, dear, you are making yourself ill."

The pain rushing through Evie's body took her breath away, and it took a while to speak. "This is what I do," she managed through gritted teeth.

Mrs Arkwright gripped Evie's arm in both hands. "I would not give you such pain. I can see it in your face and your eyes, Evie. Do not suffer for me."

"I'm all right. I simply need to—"

The door burst open and Godywn strode into the room. "What's going on here?" he asked.

Mrs Arkwright recovered first. "We're cooking, what does it look like? And I have told you—"

"Yes. Yes, you did," he interrupted. "However, you can do your cooking and this… Evie must come with me. She must earn her keep. Upstairs, not down here."

"Yes, Mr Bethwood," Evie answered.

"Good girl. Follow me."

He didn't notice that Evie drew her blouse sleeves over her hands. She didn't want him to know what she had done. It would take a few moments for the sickness to sink back into her body. A few more moments, and no one would notice.

6

_____

Bethwood jostled her out of the kitchen, up a flight of stairs, and along a passageway to a small room. An ornate washstand stood in the corner, the kind where the bowl lay inset into the top surface and lined with the finest porcelain tiles. On one side stood a jug of water and a thick bar of carbolic soap. A screen hid away one of those posh water closet things, and a flusher, too.

"Get in there," he ordered. He looked furious. "Under other circumstances, I think I would beat the shit out of you, girl, for the insolent glare in that kitchen."

Evie stared at the ground and tried to hunch over, ready for whatever happened next. Like a fist.

"Don't pull that act with me. You were going to heal that silly bitch in the kitchen, weren't you?"

Evie shook her head.

"Don't be stupid, Evie. I own you, and you only heal the ones I say. Got that?"

"Yes. Yes, sir."

"Good. You need a slapping, girl, but there is a job to be done, and I can't risk showing you as anything other than a competent healer. But later, I might not be so restrained."

"Yes, sir."

"Now you need to scrub yourself here. Mr Ellis-Wearing is a little particular about contact with people."

Evie nodded, as though she understood what such gents were like.

"All domestics especially must be clean. So scrub your hands before you go anywhere near him."

Evie scrubbed her hands with the bar of soap. She made the most of washing, not just to be fastidious, but the longer she took, the better her hands looked.

"Come on, Evie, stop faffing."

"Sir," she said.

"Let me look."

He examined her hands and nodded. "They will do. You have such rough skin, so do be cautious about inflicting your god-forgotten touch on the likes of the man you shall meet."

"I will be most circumspect."

"Good. Now, Evie, be careful, be quiet, and for God's sake, do not offend. Do well, and I may forgo your beating."

To Evie's thinking, there would be little chance of that, but she said, "Yes, sir."

"Good lass."

As soon as Bethwood opened the door, a wave of such stifling heat rolled out that it almost felt solid. Evie took a step backwards. The stench of whiskey, cigars, and stale food rode out with the heat and formed the background to something much worse. The rancid odour of sickness had strength enough to have a life of its own.

"Steady," Bethwood urged.

Evie stiffened her shoulders and let the heat roll over her. In the hearth, a fire roared at full power and threw out more heat than necessary for the time of year. Probably for any time of year.

Inside the room, and contained by the four walls, the heat grew more oppressive, like being next to a furnace. The heat seared through her nose, and the stench of sickness filled her. She opted to breathe through her mouth, and although the heat did not improve, at least the stench diminished.

She peered around the room, which seemed to be both a sitting room and a study. She saw shelves filled with books and two glass-fronted cabinets. She wasn't sure what they contained, but she saw silver and gold. Given the style of the decoration and the gold leaf, she couldn't imagine this was a cheap cabinet, and the contents were probably as expensive. Pointless, too. No one ate gold or silver. It could buy food, of course, but not when it sat in a cabinet.

In the corner, on an ornate pedestal, stood the bust of some chap with a long nose and deep-set eyes. A huge mahogany desk, larger than a bed, stood in the middle of the room and provided a home for books and papers.

A man, presumably Mr Ellis-Wearing, sat in a solid leather club chair so large and bulky it dwarfed the man who sat in it. For a moment, it looked as though the seat had started to eat and partially digest him

She stared at his face and noted the similarities between the bust and the man in the armchair. Except that the bust had more vitality to it. He wore shirt and trousers with a lounge jacket on top. If they were to have guests for dinner, Mr Ellis-Wearing did not appear ready to receive them.

Evie turned her attention to Bethwood and prepared herself for instructions.

"Alex," Bethwood said. He pushed Evie closer.

"Is that her?" the man asked. His voice had no depth to it, like a hoarse whisper forced through a closed throat.

"Yes," Bethwood replied. "This is Evie, and she will help you feel a little less discomforted."

Discomforted? This man was walking dead, but Evie

couldn't say that. "Mr Bethwood, I need to get a feel of the...the problem," she said.

"Then examine him."

Evie did not relish the task, but she had no choice. "Mr Ellis-Wearing, as Mr Bethwood said, my name is Evie Chester, and I need to examine you to see what I can do to help."

"Yes, of course, do as you must." Alex's words slurred together, and his eyes did not track her place.

"Can I see your hands?" Evie asked.

He turned his hands in his lap, and Evie could see the outline of a blotchy rash. She turned to Bethwood. "I'll need to see his back, and I'm not sure I can do this—"

"Yes, you will," Bethwood said.

"As you wish, but I'm pretty sure I can't do it in one sitting." She didn't tell him she was already at half capacity due to Mrs Arkwright. "I think he is very, very sick." Only a fool would deny that the man was so far gone it might be already too late for him.

Bethwood nodded.

He strode across the room. "Alex, I need to get your jacket off. Your shirt, too."

"All right," Alex replied, his slur more obvious now that Evie knew what to look for. She had encountered so many types of sicknesses that she might as well be a medic, or a nurse. Well, a nurse to some sickness types anyway.

"Ahh," Bethwood said.

Evie studied Alex's back, and as expected, a rash covered his skin and ran around the sides of his torso. "Ahh," agreed Evie.

"Get on with it, then." Bethwood wiped his hands on a cotton napkin, as though he would catch something by being there. Alex Ellis-Wearing had already done the catching, and this wasn't a new thing, either.

Evie glared at Bethwood. "I need to focus," she said, her

words drawn out in a hiss. "I need to be in the right place for this one."

Bethwood nodded and stepped back. If anything, Evie thought he looked relieved.

To make this man better, or at least improved, she had to think about where to draw the sickness from. Sometimes it was an all-over malady, but some attached to specific areas, and when they were this advanced, her options were limited. His options were even more limited, but she would do what she could.

She placed a hand in the middle of his back and another at the base of his neck. His skin felt clammy, probably from the heat, but she wasn't sure of that. Around his neck, his skin had a greasy, almost slimy feel, and she tried not to show her distaste.

Under her hands, she could already sense the sickness trying to escape, to go into her. She closed her eyes and let her Gift call the disease, not that she needed to make much of an appeal.

Like rats deserting a sinking ship, the infection swarmed from him to her in rushing waves. The stink of him rose up, and Evie almost gagged at the cloying and acidic sweetness. Like newly spilled vomit. It filled her mouth and coated her tongue, as though she chewed on a lump of rancid fat.

She noted, from the feel of the taint and how it affected her, that more than one kind of sickness plagued him. She had never noted that sickness, when it came to her, had different *flavours*. Not that she actually tasted the difference as such. At that moment, the thought did not mean much, but she saved it for examination later.

For now, she needed to think about the job. Alex sat there, slumped to one side as though he no longer had the will or the wherewithal to move for himself.

She examined her hands and saw streaks of black, red,

and green burrowing into her skin. They ate into her body with teeth of fire and tore into her with claws of ice.

The pain of it all took her voice away. Instead of a scream, her throat closed, and she managed nothing more than a pitiful whimper.

Evie's vision wavered and blurred as fluid seeped from the corners of her eyes. Like tears but thicker, until her eyes started to glue together. She wiped at her face, and then she saw her hands, the streaks of yellow filigreed with streaks of black. She knew without looking that sickness zipped over her face in rivulets of pollution. Even her nose had started to drip. Her purge had started. She couldn't contain any more of it.

Evie pulled her hands from Alex's skin, and for a moment or two, she could do nothing more than stand in one place as her body absorbed the disease. The effort drained her muscles, and she shook with the effort of standing upright.

She looked up and saw Bethwood.

He stood in the middle of the room with a handkerchief over his mouth. She wasn't sure if he watched with horror or fascination. Either way, he did not turn away.

"I need…" But the words would not come. She needed to be away before she purged right there on the nice, fancy, and probably very expensive rug.

Bethwood reached out and grabbed Evie's wrist as she tried to pass. "Oh no, you don't," he said.

She stopped dead when he grabbed her. "I need to go," she managed to say.

"I'll say when," he said.

Evie stared at Bethwood's hand; his big meaty fingers wrapped around her wrist as though she were nothing. She felt her insides shift. The corruption flew to the site of contact, and she began to rid herself of the taint.

Like a purge, but different.

She stared at the place where his hand touched hers; it almost didn't feel like her own skin any more. The blackness inside of her erupted through her skin and straight into Bethwood. Her Gift did not care for the barriers of skin against skin as the sickness moved from her to him without a thought.

His eyes grew wide as the shadow of the disease burrowed into him,. tendrils of purple infection writhing under his skin.

For Evie, the release of the corruption could only be described as a great relief, yet the expression on Bethwood's face did not bode well for her. He looked horrified one minute, and then his expression changed to one of fury. His face turned red. His hands clenched into fists at his sides, and beads of sweat erupted along his hair line. Fury could not withstand the pain he had to be feeling. The pain that Evie felt every time she took sickness into herself. A part of her rejoiced at what she had done, and another part knew she was in trouble.

He back-handed her with his fist, and she hit the wall so hard, she almost saw stars.

"Stupid bitch," he said.

"I need to purge," she whispered. "I can't control it when I'm so full."

"Go out the back door to Grobber, purge outside, and come straight back."

Evie didn't answer him as she opened the door and raced across the hallway to the stairs and down into the kitchen.

She didn't stop to speak but opened the back door and raced through as fast as she could. Outside, she found herself in a sunken yard. There were steps up to ground level, but a tall wall and gate surrounded the enclosure.

She saw Grobber in the yard; he sucked on the end of his hand-rolled cigarette as though he needed it to breathe. She ignored him and passed him by as though he weren't there.

"What the hell you doing here?" he asked.

Evie didn't answer. She needed to purge more than she needed to talk to the hired thug. She aimed for the far corner of the yard so that few would see and fewer would notice what she had done.

She faced the corner and looked down at her hands. She cried out as the skin split across her fingers and down the sides of her nails. Pus burst out, collected at her fingertips, and dripped to the ground in stinking splatters.

Blackened gloop oozed out of nose and mouth, and she vomited with the stench and textures of the vileness erupting from her body. She purged. All of it, all at once, and it wouldn't wait.

"What the fucking hell is that?" Grobber asked, and gagged. "What a stink."

Evie stared at the stinking mess she had made and retched. All that lovely food from Mrs Arkwright lay in a foul-smelling heap on the ground, along with the black mess that had been inside Ellis-Wearing.

She turned around when done and wiped her sleeve across her face. Mrs Arkwright stood in the light of the kitchen, her hand over her mouth. The rest of the cook's face lay in shadow, and Evie couldn't see any more of her expression.

Evie pulled back her shoulders and readied herself for the disgust and horror that would be written on Mrs Arkwright's face. People were always disgusted.

"Evie," Mrs Arkwright said.

"I'm sorry." Evie looked into her face, but she saw no revulsion, only sadness and a little pity, perhaps.

"Come on in, girl, and let's get you a cuppa."

"Yes, ma'am," she replied.

Inside the kitchen, she saw Bethwood. He stood with his hand held out, as though too disgusted at even his own skin.

"Come here, girl. You better be ready to right what you done."

A spark of anger lit inside Evie. "What I've done?" she said. "What I did was all that you asked me to do."

She walked back through the door into the kitchen. Grobber assisted her through the doorway with a none-too-gentle push against her back. She stumbled, but Mrs Arkwright was right beside her; she was there. When she had helped Evie straighten herself, the cook turned and glared at Grobber. "And you can stay outside," she said.

Bethwood did not appear at all concerned with Mrs Arkwright. He glared at Evie until her anger shrivelled up inside. She hunched over to make herself smaller.

"Evie Chester, you and I need to have a little discussion in the hallway inside." He pointed through the door. At least he didn't want to do anything to offend Mrs Arkwright.

Evie's saviour was not done. "The girl is sick. She needs to sit in the kitchen and have a cup of sweet tea before you make her do anything more. The poor lass is so unwell she had to run outside and be sick."

"She will do as she is told," Bethwood said. In this, his stern voice and sterner demeanour made his position clear. His word mattered most.

"I'm all right, Mrs Arkwright. Maybe if I do what I need to do, I can have a cup of tea afterwards," Evie said.

"Yes, you will." Mrs Arkwright nodded. "And I will feed you up again before you fade to nothing. You won't mind, will you, Mr Bethwood. This girl needs to be fed more."

He looked surprised to be a part of the conversation. "Yes, I would suppose so."

"Good. Make sure she comes to this kitchen at the earliest so I can make sure she doesn't faint away." Bethwood had almost turned away before she spoke again. "You will make sure, Mr Bethwood?"

He nodded and ushered Evie into the hallway. She flinched whenever he moved, as though at any moment he would exercise his right to be a bully. He didn't do anything. He held one hand at his side, rigid, and the other he used to stroke his chin.

He pointed at the wall. "Wait there, and do not move."

When he held up his right hand, the one he had used to grab her, she could see strings of black and purple wriggling like long worms under his skin. She had to admit, it was fascinating to watch. Almost as fascinating as the drops of sweat that lined his brow.

"What. Is. This?" he asked.

"You touched me," she answered. She hoped that would be enough.

"I did. And that means I took this from you? Or did you give it to me?"

Evie shrugged at first, but the glare from Bethwood was severe. "I don't know. Truly, I do not know. This is new to me. I think you took it, but I can't be sure. Maybe I gave it to you because I took too much of the gent's sickness."

"Very well. You will take it away, yes?"

She nodded and reached for his hand. It didn't take long, the sickness had not had time to take root, and she pulled it back without much thought.

"Done," she said.

He flexed his hand and checked every inch for blemishes. "Now then, go back to Alex, Mr Ellis-Wearing, and take more of the disease from him." He stepped closer, so close that Evie tried to step back into the wall to avoid him. "Listen to me, Evie Chester, and listen well." His breath brushed against her face in hot, fetid waves.

"Yes, sir."

He nodded and lowered his voice. "Heal him more, but do not cure. Understand me? Leave some behind."

"You want me to—"

"Yes."

"I will," she whispered.

"Good. Then afterwards, the cook can feed you up. That will save me a job."

7

The gates to the courtyard of Bethwood's house closed behind them with a loud bang. Lamplight bathed the whole walled enclosure with a pale glow.

"We're home," Bethwood said.

"Yes." It struck Evie, as she stepped out of the carriage, that Bethwood's house was a rather large one. She'd not had a chance to pay it any attention before. The size of it, the wealth he had, seemed unexpected somehow. She'd rather thought the house would be small, hidden amongst the dirtier neighbourhoods.

Bethwood ushered her inside the house and to her room. *Her* room. A luxury room, really. She had a metal-framed bed, a bedside drawer, a chair, and a lamp. It could have been worse. She could have found herself back in the pens with the others, wherever that was.

Evie noted, as Bethwood held the door for her, that someone had added a thin mattress and a thin and scratchy blanket to her bed whilst she had been out.

"I would allow you the freedom of this room inside the house, but I can't trust you. So, I either chain you here or in one of the pens," Bethwood said.

Evie remembered the pens.

"I didn't see them outside."

Bethwood chuckled. "You remember them?"

"Of course I remember." How could she not? The outbuildings were where Bethwood kept all of his more interesting 'stock,' both Gifted and not. In the pens, they were lucky to get straw to cover the damp cobbled stone flooring, and luckier still to get a blanket when it grew cold.

Better that than the old pigsty. Brick built, like the other outbuildings, but in two parts. A brick enclosure, with a lockable gate, and open to the elements. In the other half, a small shelter stood no more than waist high. A slate roof protected the pig, or the slave, from the rain, but a slave had to crawl through a small opening to get inside. The stone floor inside and out had no protection from water, and anyone locked in one of those endured a very miserable life.

Her pen, an old stable, had been home to three girls, all Gifted, and they had nothing but a small mattress and a blanket between them. The straw stayed on the floor from one month to the next, but better that than stone.

A single bucket, located in the corner near the door, provided a less than private place for necessities. The old straw had a use there, too. Sometimes they had a jug of water for washing as well as a jug for drinking water, but not often.

Evie didn't want to go back to any of those places and would do almost anything to avoid them. "This is good, better than I could wish for," she said.

Bethwood looked happy with her answer. "Good. I knew you would see the sense in it. There is a pot under the bed. Please use it."

"To cleanse myself of everything?"

"Yes." With that, he chained Evie to the bedstead and turned off all the lights on his way to the door. He paused on the threshold. "By the way, I have another client set for tomorrow. I don't want any complications. Get rested and do whatever you need to do to be ready."

Evie didn't answer. She didn't need to. Insofar as he was concerned, her agreement didn't really matter.

He closed the door behind him and plunged the room into darkness, apart from a sliver of light along the bottom of the door. After he turned the lock, she heard him walk away. After a few moments, the light under the door also went out, and Evie sat on the bed with nothing more than the darkness for company. No matter what, a bed inside a house, even with chains, was a much better proposition than the pens.

She stripped off her clothing and hung everything over the edge of the bed. The chains restricted her reach, but she managed.

Stripped to her undergarments, she lay on her bed and stared into the darkness above. The mattress, she decided, offered quite a lot of soft support. Better than the ground.

All things considered, she'd done better than she thought possible. She reminded herself of that over and over. If she said it often enough, she would forget that she had been free for a while, and now she wasn't. What had she expected? Evie Chester was a slave, and her owner had found her.

She stretched until her joints almost popped and made herself comfortable. She yawned, and before she knew it, she'd fallen asleep.

The next morning, she awoke to find fresh clothing draped over the foot of the bed. On the bedside table she also discovered a cup of tepid, weak tea and a plate with a bread roll with butter and a little jam. She considered this a feast for a Bethwood slave. She ate half of it and hid the other half, in case it was the last time he fed her.

She dressed herself in the clothing provided: a simple woollen skirt, a plain and worn blouse, and a thin jacket to go over top. She readied herself as best she could and sat at the end of her bed. Bethwood arrived soon after.

"Good morning, Evie. I have someone for you to see. Make them feel better, but do not cure."

"Yes, Mr Bethwood," she answered.

"Good. I would like to maximise your usefulness if I can."

"Of course. I will do as you wish."

So began her new routine. She would rise to find something to eat and drink, along with clean clothing. Bethwood would arrive after a while and take her to use her skill. Twice a day most days. Evie saw one or two such gents every day for a fortnight. Then back to her room to be chained up until the following day. She had been treated worse.

Bethwood was in his element. All of the clients were gents —a lord, a magistrate, a senior guardsman, and all kinds of posh city men and women. Evie said nothing controversial, did as she was bid, and kept her skills in control.

"Evie," Bethwood addressed her one morning, "we are to see my good friend Alex Ellis-Wearing today."

She tried to gauge his mood without staring at him, but she gave up. "Yes?"

"Make him feel better, girl."

"As you wish."

He laughed. "But not too well. I need his friendship for a problem that's about to arise, and it is better if he needs me as much as I need him. Understand?"

Evie nodded. "Make him feel better, but no cure."

"Exactly that. And none of that being sick everywhere. Control yourself."

Evie nodded.

The sessions with Ellis-Wearing and her other clients had proved to be great lessons for Evie. She learned, for one thing, that she could recognise her limits better and hold before she needed to purge. Secondly, the ills of the rich and well-to-do gents were no different from the cussing dockers. The fancy gent who lived in a fine house, wore fine clothes, and ate fine food, got wiener rot as much as the docker in the quayside whorehouse. Funny, that. Perhaps they should stop poking it around any place they could.

Evie learned something else, too. When she did as she was told and Bethwood smiled afterwards, then she would be fed that night. Two meals were a great bonus. It was the best she'd ever had. So much so that she even went to sleep each night without worry. Life was pretty decent, considering, and she started to take it for granted.

Pity that such a hopeful perspective didn't last much longer.

Noise, great terrifying and unexpected bangs, brought Evie from the depths of sleep to full awareness with such suddenness she thought her heart would stop. As she woke, fear clawed through her belly, and her heart pounded so hard she thought her chest would burst open. Crashes and yells followed the bangs, and a series of thuds made her cringe further. Evie drew her limbs close and scuttled backwards to wedge herself between the headboard and the wall.

Lights flashed and filled room with brightness, and the glare rendered her sightless. She shielded her eyes and waited for her vision to adjust.

"What's—" she started, but her words were interrupted when the bed shook with such violence it almost rocked on its legs and threatened to spill her over.

"Wakey, wakey," yelled someone. Bethwood? Other shadows stepped out of the brightness. She saw two men, or was it three of them? It was hard to tell.

"Get up," said a man who sounded like Grobber.

The lights moved. Still bright, but she could see a little more. Three of them. Grobber, Bethwood, and another man she did not recognise.

"Wake up, you lazy slut," Grobber yelled.

"Now, Mr Grobber, there is no need for that kind of language," Bethwood said. "Not in my house."

"Of course, my apologies, Mr Bethwood," Grobber said.

"I'm awake," Evie said. They knew that, yet the banging and the shaking took a while longer to slow down and stop.

"Good. Get dressed, Evie. We are about to see how much use you can be."

"I thought—"

"Now, Evie, don't you try any of that thinking. You'll get ahead of yourself."

The third man undid Evie's chains and pulled her off the bed by her hair. "Get up, yer lazy scummy bitch." He had a bundle of clothing in his hand, and he threw it on the bed.

Evie stared at the clothes. A long wool skirt and a shirt. Neither of them looked very clean.

"Put them on," Grobber urged. "Or we can do this with you in your under garments. Or naked." He smirked.

Bethwood and Grobber stared as she dressed. The other one went outside. He dragged in a young lad and dumped him in the middle of the room.

"Heal him," Bethwood said.

"What? What's this about?"

"Shut your hole and do as you're told," Grobber said.

Fair enough. Evie headed over to the boy, but when she lifted his chin, she found not a child, but a young man, wasted. He coughed into his hand as she touched him, and specks of blood stood bright against his pale skin. He swallowed, and his Adam's apple stood out so far it looked like a deformity all on its own. As he swallowed again, it bobbed up and down.

She stared at him. She could sense the infection in his chest, saw the wasting away of his body, and of course, the blood drops.

"Consumption?" she asked. It was a guess as much as anything, as all of her assessments were.

"Stop yakking and fix him," Bethwood demanded.

"It's all right, this will not hurt," she said to the young man. Evie lay her hands on his shoulders and called to the sickness. It came to her in lurching waves of inky blackness. She always thought of disease as an oil, like tar eating into and destroying the good in the body, and she wondered if how she imagined it was how the disease came. But she recalled the differences in Alex Ellis-Wearing. She tried to think in terms of flavours of the disease, to get an idea of how it stood out from others she'd absorbed, but as fear pounded in her chest, she couldn't sense much. Except that it was vile and the rot filled her nose and coated her mouth with the flavours and feel of mouldy bread.

Taste aside, the more she took, the healthier he appeared to be, and in that, she found some measure of comfort and satisfaction. As more of the sickness filled her, she could hear the youth take one clear breath after another. That, too, was a powerful and satisfying feeling. She saw the glow in his cheeks, the ease of his breath, and most of all, the look of relief and gratitude upon his face.

He thanked her. Not with loud words or grand gestures, but by nothing more than the wonder in his eyes and a small smile. It was enough. He knew what she had done and knew he had been given a gift.

"Done?" Bethwood asked.

Evie nodded. "I think so. I have taken all I can take."

"Don't you dare purge yourself here, girl," he said. He turned to the boy. "Well, stand up, lad. Let me get a look at you."

"Yes, sir."

"What's your name, lad?"

"Eric, sir, named after me dad."

"Well, Eric, how do you feel?"

"Well, sir. Very well. Thank you, sir. It is a gift, sir. I can breathe. Thank you."

"Do you want something to eat, Eric? You must be exhausted."

"Tired, yes, sir. But I don't want to be no trouble."

"It's no trouble." Bethwood turned to Grobber. "You go to the kitchen and get him a cup of tea, sweetened, and a slice of bread and butter or something."

"I'm no domestic serv—"

"Fetch it now, Grobber. Now."

Grobber glared but left the room. He slammed the door on his way out.

"Can't get the staff these days," Bethwood said. He grinned.

At that, Evie had the first inkling that something wasn't right. Bethwood looked even more threatening when he smiled like that.

He turned to Evie. "Stand up, Evie. Let me examine you."

She stood, and he stared at her as though he could see right inside. "I don't see the illness inside of you. Where goes this sickness?"

Evie looked at the floor. "I don't know. Sometimes you can see it on my skin, sometimes it isn't obvious."

"Really?" He looked serious now.

Even Eric stared at her as though he expected to see the sickness inside of her.

"I can't say for sure, truly, I can't, but I feel it there. Everywhere inside. I can't feel it any one place, but I can feel it."

"Hiding?"

"Perhaps."

He seemed satisfied with her answer. "Then it is like a beast? With a life of its own that isn't you?"

"I can't say for sure, but it would seem so." All she knew was that she absorbed it all and held it there until she could release it.

"Can't. Won't. No matter," Bethwood said.

"It just is," she said.

He grinned again, and Evie knew that she was not going to like whatever happened next.

"Evie, give it back to him," he said. Just like that. As though Evie held something in her hand, and he wanted her to hand it over. He didn't even care that Eric stood in the room with them.

"What?"

"Give him his sickness back."

What the hell was he thinking? "I can't," she said.

He slapped her so hard she spun on her feet and landed in a pile on the floor.

"Don't lie to me," he bellowed.

"I'm not."

"You gave me a sickness once, now do it again. I insist you do it now." He did that smiling thing. "If you don't, I'll have Eric gutted in front of you, and after, I'll force feed you his entrails." More smiling. He turned his attention to Eric. "And you can stop gawping like a fish."

Evie swallowed, hard. "I don't know how to pass it on. It's the truth. I can't force it, I've only ever done it the one time, when you were there, and that was an accident. Unintentional."

Bethwood stared at her for a moment and turned to his other associate. "Mr Wiggins, please show Evie Chester how good you are with your fists."

Mr Wiggins didn't need to be asked twice. He stepped up to the task with a great deal of fervour. Evie couldn't do anything to defend herself, and even if she had tried, it wouldn't have done any good. His blows, all solid and powerful, would leave her covered in bruises at best. She took a shuddering breath. It hurt. Hurt a lot.

"That's enough. How are we feeling, Evie?" Bethwood asked.

"Sore. I think he broke a rib," she answered.

Bethwood's swinging backhand took her by surprise. "When I want your opinion, I'll tell you what it is."

Evie stared at the floor, and not for the first time, she wished she was dead.

Bethwood pulled at his shirt cuffs to straighten them. "Now, then, let's try again, shall we?"

Grobber opened the door and brought with him a tin mug of tea and a slice of bread. He shoved both towards Eric. "Eat this," he said.

Eric looked at Evie, then at Bethwood, and then at the food.

"Eat," Bethwood instructed. "It would be rude not to, and I am not at all keen on people who are rude to me."

"Eat," Evie whispered. She closed her eyes and took a few deep and calming breaths. Her ribs hurt, but there was nothing she could do about it. "Eat," she urged him again. She stared at him. "No matter what the future holds, you might as well face it with a full belly."

Eric nodded, and Evie took that to mean he understood how serious a plight they were in.

Bethwood wiped his hands on his trousers. "Grobber, be so good as to go to the pens and bring me the fire-starter. You remember the fire-starter, don't you, Evie? What was her name again?"

"Florie." Bastard. She was only a child. Well, not so much a child as a young lass, really. She wouldn't harm anyone. "Don't. Leave her out of this," she whispered. "I'll do what I can."

"There's a girl," Bethwood said, all smug.

"I have no idea how to do what you want, but I'll try. I'll try as hard as I can."

He sat on the edge of her bed. "We have all night. Best get a start on it."

She knelt on the floor in front of Eric and wondered what she had to do. She had no idea.

She knew she was capable, because she had purged into Bethwood. Although, the more she thought about it, in that case it had been more like overflow.

Even as she thought about it, nothing much happened. She concentrated and tried various ways of pushing the illness out through her hands, but no matter how she thought about it, nothing happened.

All the way through the dark hours she tried to focus her thoughts. Bethwood said nothing. He at least seemed to accept that her skill did not naturally work this way.

She tried so hard she could feel the muscles in her face pulling. She developed a squinty eyed stared, and Eric looked terrified of her. He wasn't the only one; Evie terrified herself.

In the end, he had every right to be scared. Scared of the situation. Scared of Bethwood and his men, who seemed more inclined to violence than helpfulness. He needed to be scared of his illness, because he already knew what trouble it could bring. Most of all, he needed to be scared of her, Evie Chester, because in her hands lay the power of life and death.

Just before dawn, Evie succeeded. It wasn't so much that she knew what to do, or even how to do it. Instead, tired, fed up, and at the end of her patience, she let go of all pretence of control. She let go.

That's when she infected Eric.

She knew when he felt the rush of darkness surging back into his body. His eyes grew so wide that Evie thought they would pop out of their sockets. He didn't move, though. Fear, she could only suppose, kept him still. That and the sight of the tiny filaments of taint that burrowed into his arm.

The disease almost had a life of its own now. She could see it. The blood vessels in his arm, his neck, and his face turned black. His skin yellowed and the space around his eyes grew tinged with green.

Evie stared. She had done it. As she finished filling him

with his own sickness, his eyes rolled back into his head and he fell over.

Was he dead?

Evie sat back on her heels, frozen with horror. She looked up after a while to see Grobber watching her, and he stared at her as though she had become an incarnation of pure evil. Evie couldn't disagree. She had always thought of herself as a healer, and now she had become something far darker. She had killed with a touch.

Bethwood clapped. "I knew you would do it." He moved over to her side and stood in front of her. Even so, Evie could still see when Wiggins dragged Eric from the room.

Bethwood put his foot to Evie's shoulder and pushed. She didn't resist and toppled onto the floor.

"Now then, Evie, remember how you did that, but next time, do it faster and try not to kill them outright, eh?" He laughed.

"No," Evie said. Her voice little more than a whisper.

"No, Evie?"

"I'll not do that again," she said.

"Of course, you will. You are mine. Otherwise, I shall tell the magistrates how you killed some poor hapless lad who had done nothing wrong other than stand in your way. You will be the Angel of Death." He stopped and thought it through. "Death or mercy?" He rubbed his hands together. "Yes, I like that. Evie Chester, you will be my Angel of Mercy, and I will be the one to choose whether it is death or mercy you bring them. With you as my secret weapon, I will become the most powerful man in the city. After all, who will stand up to me when I can bring them death?"

Angel of Mercy? There were no angels.

"I killed him," she said to herself. She had taken hope and perverted it. Assassin. Murderer. She was all of these things.

Evie had crossed a line. The stain of this evil act ripped into her soul and marked it for all time. She considered herself with harsh judgement, and whatever strength she'd had vanished. She could not do this. The price of survival had risen to a cost she would not pay. Despair rose up in a thick cloud of black as dense as the sicknesses she could call. She sank into that darkness, and it swallowed her whole.

8

_____

E vie didn't move or speak when they dragged her limp body to her place on the bed, clamped the manacles around her wrists, and chained her to the bedframe. There they left her, curled up in a ball, and the sound of their laughter rang in her ears as they left.

Evie didn't care.

Her world had narrowed down to the one image that dominated her thoughts. Eric's face. She saw the hope and horror in his eyes. Such a young man, barely out of his teens, only a year or two older than Florie and a good four or five years younger than she was. Almost a child, and he'd not stood a chance to grow into the man he could have been. He'd barely had a chance to be a boy, never mind anything else.

She recalled his face etched with the pain and discomfort of his ailment. Every disease-ridden day had marked his face with lines and blemishes. She had seen those lines vanish when she'd taken away his pain. Hope had blossomed across his face to replace the pain and despair. He'd smiled, then, a radiant smile that filled the room with hopefulness. For a moment, Eric had seen the possibilities of a bright future open up in front him.

She'd given him that.

And then she'd taken it all away.

What was worse? To live a life knowing they would die, and soon? Or was it worse to feel death retreat and then have all that hope stripped away as the pain and sickness returned. To know, with absolute certainty, that death is not a looming fear but an imminent truth?

What was worse? To see hope's promise, or to see hope crushed?

Was it worse to watch someone die and realise she could do nothing? Or give someone life only to take it away? Worst of all, perhaps, was wondering whether it was better to let someone die slowly, or watch them wallow and fade in a crushing wave of pain. What was worse?

Evie knew. She had taken his disease and given it back. Not a bit at a time, as a sickness would have evolved. Instead, she'd delivered a lifetime of sickness in one fell swoop. No one could have withstood that. She might as well have stabbed him through the heart.

Evie Chester, she decided, had murdered an innocent.

T ime dragged or rushed by. Evie neither knew nor cared. Time might as well have stopped as her thoughts spiralled deeper into the darkness.

No one came to see her. Not that she remembered. She couldn't recall if she even moved. After a while, she wasn't even sure if she breathed or not. Thoughts of death and despair filled her until her soul ached. If hell existed, she was there, in spirit if not in body. This world was no longer one in which she wished to live. She gave up that night when she killed a man.

She remembered something. A thought. They say that the

spirits of the Divine Mother and the Supreme Father listen to all their children in their hour of need. Evie needed them now. She prayed in the darkness.

She didn't pray to live; she prayed to whatever powers there were that they would hold her breath in her lungs and stop her heart. Anything else would be a travesty.

As she prayed, the darkness took her, and she thought her prayers had been granted.

S omething damp and cool pressed against Evie's head. Liquid dripped over her parched and dried lips, trickled into her mouth. She swallowed. Her throat hurt, but she continued to swallow every slow drop that dribbled across her tongue. The water came quicker, too quick, and she almost coughed. Her throat closed up, and she took a deep and grating breath to steady herself.

The smell hit her then. Her nose wrinkled in disgust as she noticed a whole raft of reeking odours, none of them pleasant.

More water dripped over her lips, and she sucked it up. Too fast. This time, she couldn't stop herself from coughing.

"Steady," said a soft female voice.

She sounded familiar, too. A voice she found welcome. She listened to the sound of that voice as though it were a beacon that would draw her in.

"Wake up," the voice said.

Evie took a deep breath. It felt unwelcome and unfamiliar to the part of her that preferred to stay in the dark.

"Evie."

No matter how appealing the voice, Evie didn't want to answer or wake up. The warmth and oblivion of the darkness called her back, and Evie did not want to leave. Drops of water, like big, warm raindrops, dripped over her face. Cloth, dry and scratchy, wiped at her face and her eyes.

The drops of water came again, but this time the liquid

drizzled over her dry lips and into her mouth again. Evie couldn't help herself. She savoured those drops, and the darkness receded a little further. Sweet, refreshing drops of water.

"More," she croaked.

"Bit at a time. Can you open your eyes?"

It took a moment to remember how to do it, but she willed her eyelids to part. Her vision blurred for a moment, and a female face swam in and out of focus.

"Can you see me?" the voice asked.

Evie squinted. The face remained blurred and wavering until the image grew steady.

"Say if you can see me."

Evie didn't think she could recall how to speak. She nodded instead.

"That's good."

A few more drops of water drizzled over the corner of her mouth, and she licked them all away.

"That's better."

She recognised the woman now. "Florie?" she asked. Her voice cracked, but she forced the words out.

Florie seemed relieved. "You remember me, then."

"How could I forget?" Evie wrinkled her nose. "Something stinks."

"Yes, you."

"Thanks."

"Can you sit up?" Florie asked.

"I think so," Evie replied. Yet Florie helped her to sit up.

"I'm not in my..." Evie started.

"Not in where?"

Evie sighed. Her surroundings had changed whilst she'd succumbed to despair. She no longer lay in the place she had called her room, with the privacy it entailed. The brass bedstead had disappeared, and along with it the bedside cabinet. Instead, she lay on a thin, worn mattress on the floor. She didn't even have a blanket.

"I'm back in the pen, aren't I?"

"Of course. Where did you expect to be, Evie?"

"Nowhere," she answered.

"They dropped you here a day and a half ago, and they didn't even put you on the mattress. They left you on the stone floor."

"You took care of me, Florie?"

"Had to. I thought you were dead, or dying. You were so out of it." She paused. "What happened, Evie? You vanished into thin air!"

Even as Florie spoke, Evie still wasn't sure she was really alive. "I'm not dead then?"

"Close, Evie. No one brought you any food, or water, nothing," Florie said.

"Have they fed you, though?"

"Not since they dumped you," she said.

"Do you have more water?" Evie didn't want to ask, not when they had so little in the pens. Hunger gnawed at her belly, but the clawing dryness in her throat came close to choking her.

"I've been saving some."

"Wise, Florie."

"I saved a bit of food as well. Are you hungry?"

Evie didn't want to take her food; it was not easy to come by. "No, you need it," she answered, but her stomach growled.

"Liar." Florie smiled and pushed the hair from Evie's face. "After all you've done for me, now it's my turn to care for you."

"Truth is, I got away for a while."

"I know."

"But when Bethwood found me again, he put me in a room in his house. They kept me in a room, all on my own."

Evie sighed. "I slept in a bed, and every day I'd find fresh clothing draped over the edge of the bedframe."

"Were you dreaming? That sounds like a nice dream."

"No, it wasn't a dream, it was real."

Florie shook her head. "Never mind. Real or not, it might as well be a dream, and it's of no use to us now."

"I guess not." Evie tried not to think about how cynical Florie had become. Of all the girls she had ever encountered, Florie had always been the most optimistic of them all.

"Let's get on with more practical matters, shall we?" Florie said.

"Such as?"

"Let's get you cleaned up for a start."

For the first time, Evie noticed her dress. She still wore the clothes she'd worn when she had killed… A sob escaped her. Now she could put the dreadful aromas together. Strongest of all of them, the stinking corruption of sickness mixed with the stench of stale sweat, all blended with vomit. "You looked after me when I stank like this?"

"Of course. It was either that or leave you on the stone floor near the slop bucket," Florie answered. She grinned. "No excuses, let's get you out of these clothes."

Florie helped Evie to her feet, and together they got rid of the stinking clothing. Evie shivered in her under things, but not from the chill. Her legs felt so weak and unsteady that she wobbled a little. Florie was at her side with a steady hand. No more than a slip of a girl, but she had more strength than Evie could ever hope to muster.

"They brought your things," Florie said, and pointed at the basket of Evie's things in the corner. "They must have expected you to live."

"But they were not willing to take care of me, just in case?"

"Life is life."

"Yes, it is, Florie. Yes, it is." Even so, Evie had not expected to see any of her things again. "Clothes," she said.

Florie pulled at the items in the basket and held up a few garments. "You could do with fresh under things, too. I'll turn around if you want to strip and get you water to wash."

"Thank you," Evie answered as she started to remove her soiled and stinking clothing. "I really am grateful for all of this."

"It's all right," Florie answered.

Evie stared around the room. The old stables had once provided shelter for three horses. It was stone built, with a cobbled stone floor. The panels separating the stalls had been removed to make a larger space. The iron hay mangers had been left on the walls and underneath them were the water troughs, one for each horse that would have been kept here.

Above her head, there were exposed roof rafters where the hay loft and feed storage had been. Only a few planks remained. Small, dirt-encrusted windows ran along three walls just below the loft. Some of them could be opened, but they were all barred outside or covered with mesh.

At one end of the block stood the stable door. All wood, and split in half, with a solid lock on each door part that made certain they did not escape.

"Nothing changes, does it?" she asked.

"No," Florie agreed.

A slop bucket stood in the corner, and it was almost full of waste, mixed with straw and paper. She expected no different.

In the opposite corner, she saw a battered enamel bowl and two jugs. They were new additions. The last time she had been here, they would get a bucket of water thrown into the water troughs and that is what they would use to wash.

"All the modern conveniences, I see," Evie said.

"Yep, but we have water; that's one less job for them."

There were three mattresses on the floor, and some fairly fresh straw.

"Where's Mary?" Evie asked.

"Mary is no longer here," Florie replied. The sadness in her voice cut through her own hurt.

"Did she die?"

Florie shook her head, and the sadness in her eyes would last a lifetime. "Sold."

"Oh, Florie, I'm sorry. I know you two were close."

Florie poured a little water into the bowl. "Never mind. It is as it is, and there is nothing I can do about it."

"But—"

"It's done. Now wash yourself, Evie. You'll feel better afterwards."

Florie was right. The cool water washed away the worst of the stench that covered her hands and the filth that covered her body. There was nothing they could do about the stinking clothes other than rinse them out. Better than nothing. At least she had spares in the basket.

"You need food," Florie said.

"I do, but—"

"But nothing," Florie interrupted.

She stood on a water trough and lifted herself onto the hay manger. From there, she reached over one of the remaining loft boards. She pulled out a small leather pouch.

"Catch," she said, and threw it towards Evie. She pulled out another bag, a little larger and made of cloth.

"Where did that come from?"

Florie grinned. "When I am out working, I take what I can. Everything can have a use for us here, so I take whatever chances I get."

"Little Florie is not so little anymore."

She frowned. "I never was, Evie. None of us were."

"True."

Florie opened the two bags. "Right, I have four chunks of

bread, an apple, dried meat, and cheese." She put two slabs of bread on the side along with the apple.

"Eat what you want," Florie said. "Take all you need."

"Florie, I can't take your food."

"When was the last time you ate?"

Evie shrugged. She couldn't remember. She didn't want to remember.

"I'm not sure you can eat much at the moment. Maybe a bit of wet bread and see how you hold up?"

Evie nodded. "Probably a good idea. It would be a shame to waste food if I can't keep it down."

Florie rewrapped the food and put the bags back where she had hidden them. From a different part of the roof she recovered a couple of battered enamel cups. She filled one with water from the jug and handed it to Evie. "You probably need to drink more."

"Thank you." The bread, stale but at least not mouldy, tasted wonderful. Even so, her stomach clenched with every mouthful. "You did well to get so much food."

Florie chuckled. "I am very good at getting things."

"Good. We should save the water, though. In case they don't come back for a while."

At that, Florie laughed out loud. She pointed at a small pipe that went through a hole in the roof. "I get stuff from the foundry or where ever I work, and I have a couple of mates who help me make whatever I need. The men never search me on the way back, so it has been getting easier to sneak things in."

"Like those pipes?"

"Exactly. I rigged them up so we get a chance to top up the jug when it rains. I took a tile, got friends to make it into a plate with a hole in it and brought it back."

"If you are getting things, next time you need to bring us a key," Evie said. She wasn't joking, not exactly.

"Soon. Possibly."

Evie stared at her, but Florie wouldn't add anything to her comment.

"Anyway, regardless of all of this, thank you," Evie said.

"For?"

"Taking care of me."

"Honest, Evie, I thought you was a goner."

"Me too."

"But I spoke to you all the time. I called for you. And it worked. You came back to me."

"That must be why I'm not dead. How could I refuse you?"

"You couldn't."

"I'm glad to see you are all right here."

"Yes, it's good really. Can't complain."

Evie frowned. There was nothing good about being a slave and living in stables.

"Evie," Florie started. "What happened to you? You went away, and when you didn't come back, they were so mean to me and Mary!"

"I'm sorry. I did not mean for that to happen."

"Tell me, then, what happened?"

"A lot," Evie replied. To Evie's mind, Florie still looked too young to have to deal with these sorts of things. But slaves couldn't afford to stay young, no matter their age, and Florie was old enough now. Florie knew it, and Evie knew it. She had become a young woman who knew how the world worked.

"Well, it started the day Bethwood rented me out to those fools at the dockyard," Evie started.

"Why?"

"They were getting me to fix so much wiener pox, I thought my hands would melt off."

Florie laughed. "What happened."

"Along came these two women. One of them was dressed like a man, and—"

"No!" Florie interrupted. "She was like a man?"

"Yes, like a man. A fine suit and a swagger to show she knew who she was. She was a part of some organisation. And with her was a woman who dressed all in leather and carried a sword on her back."

"No, Evie, you're making up stories." She jumped up and sat on one of the troughs. "Tell me more."

"Am not!" Evie grinned, though. It was good to see Florie laugh and show so much interest. She leaned against the trough, almost touching Florie's knees. "I stayed in a house in Ardmore and drank tea by the fireside with someone who didn't care that I was Gifted. In fact, she thought I had been blessed."

"Blessed? Really?"

Evie nodded. "If you ever get out of here and you need to hide, go and look for the Order. They're every place, like merchants, but they are more than that. Ask for sanctuary. Ask for Magda Stoner, or Ascara."

"Who?"

Evie turned her thoughts to the two women who had been there at just the right time. "Magda Stoner and Ascara are the two women from the Order. They are the ones who saved me."

Florie gripped her hand. "We could get away one day?"

"Perhaps, yes."

"Tell me more, Evie. What were the women like?"

"Magda is tall, with hair so pale it's almost white, and her eyes are grey, maybe with a hint of pale blue. Like ice. She likes to dress like a man, and she wears it well."

"And the other one?"

"Also tall."

"Evie, in comparison with you, everyone is tall."

She chuckled. "Yes, all right, they are both tall, much taller than me, and Ascara wears leather, with a sword on her back and a pistol at her hip. She has light brown skin, dark eyes, and very dark hair. When I think of her, all I think about is sunshine."

"What was it like in the guest house?" Florie patted Evie's hand. "How did you get caught? Why didn't you go with the women?"

"I should have gone with them and joined the Order, but you know, it felt like changing one slaver for another."

Florie nodded. "I can see that. But you would have been away from here."

"I know. I didn't think clearly enough."

"What happened after that? Come on, tell me all the details."

Evie told her everything, and Florie listened as though she told the finest story. "And when I was caught, I have to admit life seemed good enough. I lived in a dream, a chained-up dream, but it was fine."

"It sounds lovely."

"It was, until Eric." As she went through all of the circumstances of his death, she could feel the darkness inside of her receding. At least a little.

"You killed him, then?" Florie asked.

"I think so."

"How? It was his sickness to start with."

"True, but I think it was because disease grows a bit at a time in the body, and I filled him all at once."

Florie held Evie's hand and leaned forward to whisper, "You know, you leaked when you were out of it."

"Leaked?"

"You know, the black stuff—the stuff you take from people."

"I leaked that?" She shook her head. "I never leak that long after a purge, and I thought I had purged everything back into Eric. That was what killed him, after all. I think."

Evie's mind wandered. Had she kept some back? Could she even do that? That was something she'd not considered.

"Whatever happened, I think what you did made you sick," Florie said. "Your eyes were yellow and gooey."

Evie scrutinised her nails for any sign of illness, but although her nails were as ragged as ever, she saw no trace of what she'd absorbed. "It sounds like I was proper sick."

"You were." Florie looked thoughtful. "I never seen you so sick, Evie. Right proper sick."

"Well, I'm all right now thanks to you."

"You know they will use you more now, Evie. You gotta be more careful. And they will use me to threaten you."

She wasn't wrong. They would use her. Bethwood was a devious beast, and he knew how to control his possessions. He'd been clever to make Florie take responsibility for her.

"You're wise for your age, Florie. Bethwood has already used you as a bargaining tool once, and he will do so again."

Florie snorted, "You think being locked in a shed is gonna keep me unwise to the ways of the people out there?"

"The world is not a good place. Not for the likes of us."

"At least we're not working on our backs," Florie said. "I'll take this job to whoring."

"True," Evie replied. Being sold by the hour, probably to dockers, would not be a pleasant thing, not for anyone.

"What will you do?" Florie asked.

"I have no idea." Evie needed to think. She had to wrap her head around the fact that she wasn't dead. Her heart still ached for Eric. "I can't kill anyone else, Florie. I can't."

"You're too soft, Evie, and you will not be rewarded for it."

"Is it wrong to feel compassion?"

"Here? Evie, look where we are. Of course it's wrong," she answered.

· · ·

T he next day, two of Bethwood's men opened the top half of the door, checked where Evie and Florie were, and opened the bottom half.

"Get back," one of them barked. His voice was slurred with the dialect of the farms to the south west.

Evie had no intention of approaching them, and neither did Florie by the way she sat against the wall farthest from the door.

"We don't wanna be catching no witch shit from you," slurred the other.

Evie sighed, but didn't respond.

They slid a box across the floor. Neither of them stepped inside the building.

"You can come in," Evie said. "We will stay over here if you like."

One grunted and took away the slop bucket, replacing it with an empty one. He grunted again, and this time he pushed a jug of water into the room. He didn't touch anything else and didn't take away the other jug.

The door slammed shut, the locks were reapplied, and they heard nothing more.

"Guess they didn't want to get too close," Evie said.

"I know. I thought the one looked terrified." Florie laughed. "Good."

"Not if we want them to bring us food."

"They will. Put what we don't want near the door and anything we want to keep, put as far away as we can. We have three jugs now. That makes saving water easier."

Evie had to agree.

"Anyway, what's in the box?" Florie asked. She sounded happy as they went to peek inside. Like she was getting a gift.

"You open it," Evie said.

Inside, on the top, rested two bowls covered with tin lids and surrounded by two thin blankets. Evie wondered if they were to keep the bowls upright, or because the night air could be chilly even at this time of year. She found two spoons, too. To that they had added half a loaf, and although a little on the stale side, it would last a few days at least. A thick slice of cheese the size of Florie's hand and almost as thick as one of her fingers sat under one bowl, and inside a waxed paper pocket were dried apple rings. Luxury.

Evie opened one of the lid tops, and inside, the bowls contained a thin but cold soup. Fat had congealed around the rim, and it didn't look too appetising. Florie cooed as though they had been given more money than she could carry.

"How long will it have to last do you think?" Evie asked.

Florie shrugged. "Drops like this are not often. I've only had cheese once."

"We should eat well now, and if we get a chance to grab more when we go outside, take whatever we can get a hold of."

"Yes."

Evie looked at the cool soup. Soup? More like dirty dishwater, but she was hungry.

"It's a feast," said Florie.

Evie didn't tell her about all the food she'd had from Agatha at the guest house or Mrs Arkwright at the Ellis-Wearing house. Sometimes it was good to hear of another's fortune, and sometimes it broke one's heart.

"Wish it was hot, though," Evie said.

"You want it hot? I can make it hot."

"Now, Florie, the last time you tried to do that, you almost made the stable roof explode."

Florie laughed, and Evie found herself smiling with her.

"I know, I know."

"If you burn the shed, we'll be locked inside and roasted."

"Watch this. I've been practicing."

Florie placed one of the bowls in the middle of the floor and wrapped her hands around the outside. She closed her eyes, and nothing seemed to happen at first.

For a while, Evie thought that nothing would happen at all. Then the aroma of soup rose up and filled the shed. She passed Evie the bowl, and it was hot. Almost too hot. She repeated the process for her own bowl.

"Blimey, Florie, I'm impressed. I had no idea you could do this. How'd you learn?"

"I know. I was talking to Sim when—"

"Sim? Who is this Sim?"

"He's a lad on the engines at the Mill Works. They call 'im Simple, you know, cos his name is Simon. Simple Simon. Sim."

"All right."

Evie put down her bowl of hot soup and listened to what Florie had to say.

"Anyway, we were talking about fire and heat and things, and we got to talking about using the Gift in more ways than making a fire."

"You told him about your Gift?"

"Yeah, he's a good lad. Sim says it may be that I can focus some kind of heat in one place, and I add more and more until it makes fire." She shrugged. "Doesn't make sense to me, but if I think and concentrate on what I want, it seems to happen more often than not."

"The more control you have, the better it will be."

"I know." Florie fiddled with her fingers. "He's teaching me things, and makes sure I get food when he sees me."

Evie nodded. "Food is good, but what is he teaching you, other than a way to understand your Gift?"

Florie put her bowl to one side and lifted her foot across her other leg. She fiddled with the heel of her rather scuffed boot and peeled back a section. Inside she pulled out a piece of thin wire.

"What's that for?" Evie asked.

"Sim's teaching me to pick locks and stuff. We're making tools and hiding them in my boot. I need a couple of more pieces yet. They need to be the right size for my hands and my skills. I need to spend time practicing on the locks he finds."

"Is this the way to get around the locks here, then? You don't need a key, just the picks?"

"Yeah. I can't get away when I'm working, so it has to be when we're alone. Wiggins is always there, and he's aching to find some excuse to hit me."

Evie shivered.

Florie stared into Evie's eyes. "Are you all right, Evie?"

"What? Why?"

"I worry about you. And that shiver was pretty heartfelt. Have you met Wiggins before?"

"I have. Be careful of him. He's a vile man and will take joy in causing you pain."

"I know that. He's sick in the head, that one," Florie answered. "I think he gets excited by beating up women."

"You're right. I think he does at that."

Florie patted Evie's knee. It seemed such a mature and thoughtful thing to do. "Come on, there's more you aren't saying. I know you, Evie, you can't hide from me. Talking of Wiggins reminded you of something. Did he do something?"

"Can't keep secrets from the likes of you, now, can I?"

"No. Spill the secrets."

"I'm not sure I can. And I am not sure I should."

"Evie."

She held up one hand to stop Florie but said nothing for a moment or two. Her thoughts whirred with memories, most of them unpleasant.

"It's not about Wiggins as such, but he was there. Wiggins, Grobber, and Bethwood," she said. "I couldn't live with what I had done, Florie." She sat back against the wall and drew her knees up against her chest.

"Yes, all of them are horrible, I know," Florie said.

"I don't think you do."

"I do," Florie said. "I saw the bruises all over you, Evie. I know what causes them."

Evie stared at her hands. She had not given the bruises that covered them a thought until now. They were healing; she didn't need to dwell on it. "You're right. I was encouraged."

"Bet it was Wiggins, too."

"Doesn't matter. The bruises are nothing, but mention of him reminded me of Eric. After what I did to him, I sank into such despair, I couldn't even stir from my sleep."

"You were sick, Evie."

"I don't get sick, Florie."

"You were sick in your heart, and even you can't fight that off."

"Perhaps." She had a point, though. If she had been leaking, she hadn't been as well as she might have been. She assumed she had emptied herself back into Eric, but what if she hadn't? "I'd given up, Florie. I'd given up the will to live."

Florie squeezed her knee once more. "No, you were tired and sick. I cared for you when you were sick, and you got better. What more is there?"

Evie shook her head. Florie, who had so little, had given her all she had. That selflessness shamed Evie to the core. "You saved me, and I am grateful to be alive."

"Silly, I did nothing."

"No, it was everything," Evie said. She placed her hand on Florie's and squeezed. "You cared for someone who looked fit to die, and you shared your last food with her."

"Of course. I would share everything I had with you."

"Even though I can't promise to give you anything back?"

"Silly Evie, you have always taken care of me. It's only right I take care of you."

"Thank you," Evie said. "Thank you for taking care of me.

Thank you for being here, and thank you for restoring my soul."

In her heart, she made Florie a promise: they would survive this place, this life. Together. Evie kept this promise to herself, though, because to speak it would jinx it, and she would do everything she could to make sure she kept her word.

Evie picked up her bowl and took a sip of soup. Florie copied her. Evie broke the loaf in half. "Put this away for later, Florie, in case this is all we have."

She broke the remaining piece into two halves, which she shared between them. They ate hot soup and stale bread whilst they sat, shoulder to shoulder, in companionable silence.

It was divine.

9

_____

Their isolation in the pen worried Evie. On the one hand, the longer they were left alone, the better. It meant they wouldn't be asked to do anything unpleasant. On the other, the longer they were left, the less their value.

The silence didn't make sense.

Florie hadn't worked a day whilst Evie had been sick, which didn't sound like Bethwood at all. Under more normal circumstances, Florie would have worked every day, no matter how unwell Evie had been.

Unless he considered their usefulness at an end.

In which case, at best, they would be sold; at worst, they were a liability. Evie didn't want to finish that thought. Right then, Evie dreaded the moment when Bethwood remembered they existed.

She didn't have long to wait for their isolation and uncertainty to end. A few hours later, she heard the clicks and clunks of the padlocks on the door being opened.

"The guards must have told him I was awake," Evie said.

"Probably. Now we will be made to work again," Florie agreed.

"Well, Bethwood doesn't like to let his assets go to waste."

It wasn't a guard who came to them, but Bethwood himself. Although he was a big man, more than big enough to overpower two women, he brought two others with him, and they filled the whole shed with their importance.

Bethwood glanced around, and his nose wrinkled with distaste. He pulled a white cotton handkerchief from his pocket and covered his nose and mouth. His gaze settled on Evie and Florie as they huddled together on their mattress.

"I'm glad to see you up and about, Evie," he said. "I have work for you to do."

Evie thought he might. "Must be important for you to be here yourself."

He pointed at Florie. "You, girl, come here."

Florie did as bid, as she must, and stood before him, her gaze cast downward. She rarely had bruises, so Evie knew Florie followed her orders without question.

He turned his attention back to Evie. "Now then, we are going to the house of a friend of mine. You will heal him. Mostly."

Not much of a friend, then.

"You will keep the sickness, as you did before, and no ridding yourself of it," he continued.

"Whatever you want." She could do that.

"I trust you know the limits of what you can take?"

"Yes, Mr Bethwood."

"Good. After that, I have someone I want you to infect."

"No."

"Yes, Evie." He grabbed Florie by the back of her neck. She was little more than a slip of a thing, and he was so large his hands almost circled her neck. Florie didn't move, but her eyes grew wide. "If you refuse, I can tell you this, you will be allowed to go to her funeral, you shall see her in an open casket, and watch as we throw her remains into a hessian sack and throw her into a paupers grave."

Evie ground her teeth together and hoped Bethwood did not see the effect his words had on her.

Florie noticed, though. "It's all right, Evie, you do what you think is right," she said. "None of this is your fault. You know this. Follow your heart and soul. Do what is right."

Such a wise head on shoulders so young.

Bethwood kept his hands on Florie. He tightened his grip and squeezed until she winced. He smiled at the sound of her discomfort and squeezed her neck so hard, she closed her eyes in pain. "Never mind, Evie. I do understand your dilemma," he said. "Truly, I do. You have a gift, and you do not like to use it on those you consider innocent. Then let's try this, you will only have to infect those who are guilty of some unpleasantness or another."

"You would ask me to judge whether a person should live or die? Or will you do the judging?"

"You will not have to judge them, and neither will I. We will let the judiciary decide. We will gain access to some wrong doer, one already convicted of great crimes. Your recipient is to be a convicted criminal."

Evie didn't respond.

"You are mine, Evie Chester, don't you forget this. I wish you to learn the full power of your gift, and you will practice how to make people sick without killing them. The price of your rebellion will be mirrored in the pain we inflict—not on you but on little Florie here."

"I see." Evie narrowed her eyes.

Bethwood had not finished. "Today, you will take the pox from a friend of mine. More of an acquaintance, really, but I have a use for the man. When you are done, we will take this sickness and you will give it all to a man who is guilty of many crimes. Right now, he sits on Dead Man's Row at the prison and is awaiting an appointment at the gallows. Will you do this?"

Evie glared at him for a moment. His hand remained

around Florie's neck, and the threat remained. What choice did she have? Evie turned her gaze to Florie.

Florie smiled. "It's all right, Evie."

Evie closed her eyes for a moment to allow her thoughts to settle. She could not risk Florie. She meant too much. She'd brought hope to Evie when she'd none left.

Besides, she had a promise to keep. Florie had shown her that she could learn more about her gift. As Florie controlled hers, Evie wondered if she could learn to do the same, or at least control it better. Agatha Hickman had implied the same thing. Maybe their escape would be possible only as a result of how they used their gifts. For now, Bethwood was giving her the opportunity to practice.

"All right. You give me no choice. I will do this."

He nodded once and let Florie go. A man brought in fresh clothing. They did not fit Evie well, but they were clean and functional.

"By the way, young Florie here will accompany you on every trip. In case you are worried for her welfare, Mr Grobber will be with us, and he shall make sure that no ill befalls the young lady."

B ethwood chose a larger carriage for this trip. The four-wheeled and fully enclosed cabin had space for four. Grobber sat on the outside of the carriage, as did the driver and the coachman.

They rattled through the wide avenues and narrow streets of the city. They drove through the steam and smoke of the docklands and beyond the bangs and crashes of the factories.

A large airship, of the cargo-carrying kind, flew overhead, and for a moment Evie remembered Agatha. She would have to get word to her at some point. At the very least, she needed to thank her again for her kindness. One day, she promised. One day.

They drove through the suburban districts to the southeast. Here the roads became wider and less frequented. The houses grew larger, and the spaces between them vaster.

Brick and stone made way for the greenery and clean skies of the country. Rich folk all seemed to like their green and open spaces and the chance to get as far as possible from the stench of the people who made them rich.

Florie didn't seem to pay attention to the scenery. She stared at the upholstery on the seat opposite. She had no interest in anything.

"I'm sorry," she whispered over and over.

Evie held Florie's hand. "It's not your fault, Florie. Don't fret, it will all work out for the best."

"Will it?"

Evie forced a smile across her face. "I promise."

Florie nodded, but she continued to stare into the seat as though unconvinced.

Evie couldn't say or do anything more reassuring, so she turned her attention to the outside world and stared through the small window at her side. She liked to look at all the fine houses as they drove by and imagine what they were like inside. She made up pictures in her head of all the fancy furniture and dozens of servants who did everything for the people who lived there. A dream life.

An hour or so later, they pulled off the road. A private drive ran a good half mile or so to a wide turning area. The grounds of this house were extensive and so vast that she saw teams of gardeners tending to the plants.

The house itself, large by any standards that Evie could conceive, stood dark and menacing. Three storeys high, with dozens of narrow windows and almost as many chimney stacks.

Bethwood cleared his throat and straightened the cuff on his shirt. "We're here, so best behaviour. Remember what I told you."

"I remember," Evie said.

"And that is?"

"Take most of the sickness, or as much as I can hold, but not all, hold it inside, and no purging."

He nodded. "Good. Don't, let me down."

The door to the carriage opened, and a young man in a double-breasted coat, waistcoat, trousers, and small black tie stood to one side. "Good day, sir."

"Godwyn Bethwood. I think you'll find I'm expected."

"Indeed, you are, sir. If you would be so kind as to follow me, I'll show you inside."

Bethwood rose up, and the carriage creaked and listed as he exited. Evie followed. As Florie got to her feet, Bethwood waved her back. "You stay here. Mr Grobber is here to ensure your safety."

He turned to Grobber. "In a few minutes, escort the kid to the kitchens at the rear. Get yourself a cup of tea if you can, and wait for us there."

"Lay a hand on her, *Grobber*, and I'll see how you fair when I touch you," Evie said through clenched teeth.

Bethwood nodded. "Good point, Evie, and I'd let you, too. If fact, it would be a most interesting encounter."

I nside, the house displayed more finery than Evie could ever imagine. Even more than the Ellis-Wearing house, but in a different way. That house was cluttered and ostentatious. This house had less on show, but to Evie, it meant that these pieces were so important they could not be hidden in the shadows of other art.

She saw lots of paintings. Portraits of heads and shoulders —family, she supposed—and pictures so huge they stood taller than she was. She saw horses and hunting, vast landscapes, and buildings she could barely imagine.

It looked spooky to Evie. One of the pictures seemed to

stare at her as she walked through the house. Almost as if the paintings themselves knew that she had no place in a house such as this.

The footman showed them through to a room larger than most houses Evie had ever stepped inside. The gent, the man who lived here, stood beside a large ornate fireplace. Unlike most fireplaces, this one had been carved out of black slate. Evie had heard of such a thing, but she had never seen the like until that very moment.

Big, black, and ostentatious, it suited this place and the pinched-faced shrimp who stood beside it.

"Mr Bethwood, is this her?" he asked, as they came through the door. He didn't pay attention to Evie.

"It is, sir."

The man held out his hand, his fingers limp, as though he'd stuck them in something unpleasant. He looked away as though he would catch something even less pleasant should he catch sight of her.

"Well, go on, Evie, do your thing," Bethwood urged.

"I usually—"

"Do it," Bethwood insisted.

Evie grabbed the man's hand and waited to see what responded to her gift. The sickness in him seemed slight, and she called out to his affliction. Not that Evie could claim herself to be a medic of any standing, but she sensed that this man had little infection to worry about. Nonetheless, she called to the disease and absorbed a portion as required, whilst leaving a little behind.

The man barely registered her presence, and when he did, he turned his mouth up in a sneer. The look made her feel worth less than shit on his shoe. For a moment, she wished she had saved some of Eric's disease and fed that back to him.

She smiled, though, for Bethwood's benefit. "There you go. I have taken what I can. Good job, too. Given another few days, Mr Piper down there would have been less than a nubbin." She turned away, and winked at Bethwood.

The man at the fireplace rang a small bell that barely made any sound. The footman must have been right outside the door, however, because he came immediately. The man gestured towards Evie. "Kitchen," he said.

Bethwood followed her outside. "Evie, did you do as I asked?

Evie curtsied. "Yes, sir, absolutely as you asked."

He smiled. "Good girl. I will meet you in the kitchen in a moment."

Bethwood returned to the room to speak, she assumed, with the man of the house. Evie never caught his name, and she didn't really care.

She found Florie and Grobber, and they all drank a cup of tea together in a most civilised way. The domestic staff were not as nice and generous as Mrs Arkwright had been. They didn't speak with them, but their manner, although a little standoffish, was not a problem.

She wanted to call them snobs, but then again, if they'd been told to expect Gifted people, that could affect how they were behaving. After all, no one wanted to catch that kind of strangeness.

It was also possible that their fear of the strange was the reason they didn't say a word when Florie let some fruitcake and an apple fall into her pocket.

Good lass, Florie. Evie tried not to stare, and walked in the opposite direction. She lifted a plate, and before she knew it, the kitchen staff were all around her, making sure she didn't infect the china or something.

When she turned back, Florie grinned, and Evie wondered at what else she had taken. She was far too comfortable with that light-fingered business for this to have been her first attempt. Maybe Simple Simon had taught her more than the nature of heat and the basics of lock picking.

Evie grinned back and added an apple of her own. She also took a small chunk of bread that she found in the pantry. It was fresh, too. She thought about some cheese but couldn't find a knife. A whole wheel of hard cheese under her skirt would have aroused suspicion.

They didn't wait for Bethwood. Grobber ushered them back to the coach after a short time, and Florie grinned all the way. She carried on smiling even when he gave her such a push that she almost fell over. Nothing, not even a bully, could dent her good mood.

Bethwood joined them almost as soon as they were inside the coach. "Are you ready to unload your gift?" he asked.

Evie nodded. "He was not as sick as the others. I am not filled near to bursting."

"You left some sick behind, though, didn't you?"

"Yes. It was hard as he had so little."

"Good." He used his walking stick to bang the roof of the coach, and the vehicle lurched as they set off. "I liked what you said in there, but he was annoyed at your impertinence."

Evie shrugged. "Horrid little man."

"I can't disagree, Evie, but he is an important horrid little man."

"Who now thinks he owes you," Evie said.

Bethwood glared at her for a moment, and he nodded. "Yes, he does."

After that, they spoke not a word as they headed back. In the distance, the smoke of the city rose up in waves of black, and every mile brought the blackness a little closer.

Airships and dirigibles flew this way and that, and from where Evie sat, the ships were no more than the size of flies buzzing as lively as they would around rotted fruit. It seemed an appropriate thought for such a place as Bristelle.

Once in the city, they didn't go directly back to the Bethwood residence. Instead, they clattered through the dark streets around the docks and went down the main street to

Stake Island. There could be no mistaking their destination, and Evie shivered at the thought of the place.

Stake Island, or The Stake, was not a place to visit on a whim. Once most people went in, they only came out in a box or a sack.

Here, the dirty waters of the river grew widest. In the middle of the waterway stood the thin stretch of land known as Stake Island. The dull rock of the island sprouted two buildings at either end of the land and looked like some grey-horned devil rising from the water. The two horns were the twin gaols of The Stake.

On the right bank of the waterway, the docks had once been used to build the biggest ships. Bristelle docks had been renowned for shipbuilding. Now the docks offered nothing but a grime-covered memory of those glory days. To the left, the cobbled road turned and followed the river bank to a spit of land that formed a barrier between the river and the rotting, slime-covered wharfs of the old canals. They, too, had once been a major transportation system throughout Mid-Angle.

But they turned neither left nor right, heading instead for the bridge that crossed over to Stake Island. To the west end of Stake island stood a dark and misery-filled black stone building.

"That's Whore's Wood, the women's prison," Bethwood said.

Evie shivered.

"Once, so far in the past it's almost lost from memory, there used to be woods on that very spot," Bethwood added.

Evie didn't think trees would ever wish to grow on such a miserable spot.

He pointed to the eastern end of the island where a much larger building loomed. "Felon's Court," he said.

"I bet they have no history of anything nice there," Evie said.

"Right. It was Hangman's Corner for a while." Bethwood grinned. "They had gibbets over the water, and when the prisoners were dead, they cut the rope and dropped them in."

"And the walled area between them?" Florie asked.

"Executioner's Yard," Bethwood answered.

Evie had heard of the yard, and now she saw it for herself. It was a substantial area, large enough to house a good-sized crowd. And at a penny a go to watch, it was quite a money spinner for the prison. It was said that when the great train robber Robert the Wag got caught, there were three hundred people squeezed into the hanging yard to watch.

The carriage stopped before the river. Bethwood opened the window and scanned the sides of the river until he found what he sought. "Signal the guards to let the bridge down. We're expected," he yelled.

Evie shivered as the coach rattled over the narrow bridge. The guards who had lowered it raised it almost as soon as they crossed. Two guards approached the carriage, checked who they were, and waved them over to the gaol.

Evie's heart pounded in her chest. She worried, after all they had done, whether Bethwood had decided to get rid of them by having them imprisoned. She would not put it past him. Florie must have felt the same; she held onto Evie's hand and squeezed.

The coach turned, though, and headed towards the carriage park next to Felon's Court, not Whore's Wood. As they stopped, a dozen armed men surrounded the carriage.

Bethwood opened the window and called out to the nearest one. "Good man, we are expected. Please inform Governor Davies that Godwyn Bethwood and Evie Chester have arrived."

"You are expected," the guard called back. "Stay where you are."

One of the men jogged into the building, and a few minutes later, a rather portly chap walked up to the carriage.

He did not approach the coach, but after a nod, one of the guards opened the carriage door. "Godwyn. This way," he said.

"Governor Davies, let me show you Evie Chester."

The man looked Evie up and down. "Slip of a thing, eh, Godwyn?"

Bethwood laughed. "Lead on, my friend, lead on. Grobber here will stay in the carriage with young Florie."

"Remember," Evie said to Grobber.

From there, the governor led them into the front hallway of the administrative centre of the prison. As soon as they entered, Evie's mouth filled with the bitter taste of misery and death. This was not a nice place to be. Even less pleasant than their old stables.

"Bethwood, I'd almost given up on you." He rubbed his hands together as though cold. It wasn't the warmest of places, and Evie knew that this arrangement, or anything like it, was probably not common.

"You shouldn't have. We made an agreement."

"Indeed we did. How are matters progressing?"

Bethwood nodded. "As expected."

"It is not unusual to allow experimentation on the prison populace. However, the nature of our situation is exceptional," the governor said. He kept staring at Evie, and she wanted to jump up and say boo to see if he would jump.

"The benefits will far outweigh any risks you might incur," Bethwood answered.

"This is true, but I would rather it did not become commonplace gossip," the governor said.

"Neither would I," Bethwood agreed. "Neither would I. Value can only be gained if no one else tries to replicate what we are trying to do."

"Quite. Discretion is assured?"

"Of course."

The governor and Bethwood led the way, and Evie

followed along with two guards to the rear. They tramped through a series of dank corridors to heavy iron-bound doors, with iron rivets as large as the diameter of Evie's finger and a small hatch the guards could peer through.

There were lots of cell doors on either side of the corridors they walked along, and every so often they came to a section door. As they approached each of these section doors, one of the guards at the rear of their group called out, "Governor approaches."

The hatch in the door opened up, a pair of eyes looked out, and they heard the sounds of the mechanism as the locks clanked. The doors were pulled open with a squeal of badly maintained hinges. At each door were two guards, and they stood to the side, cudgels in hand, as the party passed by.

"Good man," the governor said as he passed them, and then the doors clanged shut and they were locked in the next section. Door after door, they passed, and the routine remained the same for each one.

Beyond each gate, Evie heard the sound of incarcerated misery echo from every wall. She shivered, not just from the chill of the cool corridors, but with the gloom and sorrow that filled every space. She hoped, with every fibre of her being, that she would never end up in a place like this.

They governor stopped outside a door made of what looked to be solid metal.

The governor coughed into his hand. "Here we are. Executioner's block, or Dead Man's Row, call it what you will. The men here are all marked for hanging, and they get to stay here until the time of their death." He banged on the door, and a narrow view panel at eye level slid open.

All at once, a wall of sound seemed to burst from the panel. The sound of people coughing, chains clanking, and the echoes of lives even more miserable than the one Evie led.

"Governor Davies," a rough voice said.

"Open up. These good people are here to pay a visit to one of our most esteemed residents."

There was a rasp of bolts being drawn back. Then came a heavy and tortuous screech as the locking mechanisms were drawn open. With a squeal that a touch of oil might fix, the door swung inwards. The guards ushered them through into the next area, and the *thunk* as they closed and locked the door behind them sounded rather loud and final.

If Evie thought the noise bad, the smell that rolled out was ten times worse. The stench had become so thick, it almost had form. Bethwood and the governor raised handkerchiefs to cover nose and mouth. Evie had nothing. She hoped they didn't catch anything as they stepped through the stink of human misery to the cells at the back.

"This way," said the guard, and led he them into the depths of the section. They stood in a square room, almost like a yard but covered and surrounded on each side by numerous gates made of iron bars.

He escorted them to one such gate in the farthest corner. "This one."

He unlocked the gate with a *clank*, and the door swung open with a screech. Inside, the floors were wet and stank of filth and misery. Evie almost gagged at the reek.

A man hunkered down on his slab of stone and ignored them. He wore a dirty shirt and even dirtier breeches. His bare feet were covered in filth and sores.

Evie, who knew about being locked up, looked at the state of his cell. He had no slop bucket for a start, and no bowl for water or other amenities. His waste littered the floor.

The guard pointed at the man inside. "That's the one."

"Excellent," Bethwood replied.

"I will leave you to it," Governor Davies said. He turned to one of the guards. "When they're done, escort them to the main offices so I can have a last word."

"Yes, of course, sir," he answered.

Davies said nothing more as he left. He'd done his part and no sensible person would stay unless they had to.

Bethwood waited until the guard stepped away before he addressed the condemned man. "Mr Vaughn, I believe your time on this earth is limited, is it not?"

"What's it to you?" he replied.

"You are convicted of murder and molestation of those who could not say no, correct?"

"Convicted, yes. Now fuck off and leave me alone."

Bethwood lowered his handkerchief. "See, Evie? I am as good as my word."

"Did you do it?" she asked Vaughn.

"I'll do you, if you like. Show you what it's like."

"Hold your hand out, then, if you want a nice gift before you go," Evie said. The fool did.

She called the taint and realised she'd nurtured this sickness like a child would hold a puppy. Closer to her body, and gathered together, ready for whatever she wished. She had not thought she could do that, but sometimes her Gift seemed to respond to what she wanted almost as much as what she needed. She was taking control of her skill. She considered this and saved the thought for examination later.

"Here I go," she said. She touched the back of his hand with a single finger and purged. It did not feel the same as her usual purge. Her skin did not split, and her nails didn't turn funny or grow painful. It was more that the disease crossed from her to him without any of the nastiness. She liked that aspect of the process.

She stopped when she was halfway done, and when she was satisfied that she had complete control, she unloaded the rest of the sickness into him.

Almost all. She didn't have much to spare, but she kept a little back, and a tiny kernel of the taint and corruption coiled in on itself and lay still and dormant. Evie smiled to herself. So far, so good.

She turned her attention to the prisoner and watched as the corruption blossomed into a black blister. She had not expected that. Nor had she expected the purge to contain so much.

It hurt him, this prisoner. He screamed, and the black blister fractured inside his skin. Eve watched as the worms of taint burrowed out from the infection site and into him.

"Spectacular," Bethwood said.

Evie agreed, and she wondered if purging through a single finger had focused all the corruption into one spot. It was an interesting thought.

Evie wiped her finger on her skirt now that she'd finished. "Vaughn, you'll never do anything wrong to anyone again. Come tomorrow morning, your dick'll fall off, and you'll have to piss through your nose." She turned around and walked away. She'd done her thing; there was no reason to stay any longer than needed.

Bethwood sniggered. "Evie Chester, you have a foul mouth on you."

She shrugged.

"It is appropriate, though, and I'll not blame you for your baseness. Not today."

The guard took them back through the gate and all the way to the administration area. Bethwood strode at her side the whole time.

"Here we are, through here, and if you take a seat in the waiting room, the governor will be out to see you soon."

Bethwood said nothing until the guard had left. "You have the hang of it now?" he asked.

"I think so, but I wasn't full. Still, it was a useful experiment." She never mentioned anything about the sickness she kept.

"Good. I need a word with the governor before we go. When he arrives, you can go outside to the carriage and wait there with Grobber and Florie."

"Of course." Evie didn't care. Bethwood looked very happy, and if he was happy, she and Florie would be left alone.

His happiness didn't diminish even when the two women were returned to their pen. Bethwood sent them hot tea and hot stew with meat in it.

Meat!

A feast was what it was. A feast.

10

E vie and Florie sat side by side on the mattress as they ate in quiet and contemplative silence. Evie had much to consider, but her thoughts were distracted by the broad grin on Florie's face.

Evie finished her food and placed the bowl on the floor. "Come on, spill it. What's got you grinning like a cat with a bowl full of cream to herself?"

"Nothing."

"There is absolutely something." Evie waved her hand in Florie's direction. "I saw, you know."

"Saw what?"

"Don't play the innocent with me, Florie. I saw you pocket some things."

"Oh!" Florie looked disappointed at first, her eyes narrowed. "I don't think you did."

"Yes, Florie. An apple and some fruitcake. I saw."

She dug her hands into her skirts and pulled out the apple and the fruitcake.

"You were good," Evie said.

"Not good enough, if you saw."

"I was lucky to see it, and I knew what I was looking for."

Florie laughed. "But you didn't see this." She pulled out two delicate little bread rolls. They were so soft and fresh, it would be days before they went stale. "And there is this." This time, she pulled out a napkin, which covered a thick slab of meat pie covered in thick pastry. She finished her showing with two fresh eggs.

"A feast," Evie said.

"That is how I can get a little extra stored here," Florie said.

"Don't be smug."

"Why not? I'm getting good at this," she said.

"Florie, be careful. They could hang you for this, and if nothing else, that visit to Stake Island should make you beware."

"Only if they catch me."

"Just be careful."

The next day, Bethwood fed them again. A thin soup this time, with buttered bread and a jug of weak tea. It made a nice change from water.

"We should save some of this food and stuff," Evie said.

Florie shrugged. "We're being fed well because of you. Make the most of it, I say."

"But it might not last."

"Doesn't matter. This is good. We have food. At least we're not getting a thrashing, and we're being fed every day even though we haven't been out to do any work in two days. This is as good as it gets, Evie."

"Florie, we live in a stable and sleep on a thin mattress with straw on the floor. We are forced to do things we don't want to do and often don't even get good food in exchange."

"It's better than it was, and better than it could be," Florie replied.

"No, Florie, it isn't. We should not live like this."

"If you say so, but I've been there when the mob came for

me. It is better to live like this than be ripped apart by a crowd that doesn't understand who and what we are."

Evie thought about that. "Perhaps."

They sat in silence for a while before Florie spoke. "Evie, have you ever wondered what it would be like to be, you know, normal?"

"What, without the Gifts we were given?" Evie asked.

"Yes, maybe."

"Why? Why ask about something that cannot be?"

"I don't know. We could live in a house, find husbands, get married, and be normal."

"Are you thinking about your friend Simple Simon?"

Florie laughed. "Who's to say."

Evie shook her head. "As to your question, no, I've never wondered," she lied. Many times, she had wished she could have been born the same as everyone else. A child without a Gift. A mundane person, like everyone else. "Why would I waste time dreaming about what cannot be?"

"Don't you want to get married?"

"Even Gifted people get married, Florie. I don't need to be without a Gift for that." As she spoke, Evie wondered if that were true. Would she want to touch anyone or be touched when she would always take their sickness? She shook the thought off.

Florie picked at a scab on her knuckle. "It'll never happen, though, will it?"

"Never say never." Evie reminded herself of her promise. They would get away one day, and she would give Florie the normal life she wanted. "Right now, we are alive."

Florie shrugged. "And we live in a pen."

"For the moment," Evie said. "But right now, I would be more concerned with Bethwood's surge in goodwill."

"Why?"

"Because everything has a price."

"And our fortune will change."

"Yes, that's what I worry about."

Evie didn't wish to upset Florie any more than she needed to. Her thoughts darkened, but she kept them to herself.

Instead, they spent the rest of the day making plans for a life they would never lead, and reminisced over the good moments they'd had.

L ater that night, a storm hit Bristelle. Not a bad one, but the winds picked up, the temperature dropped, and the rain fell so hard it sounded like thousands of rocks drummed against the roof for three hours or more.

The roof didn't leak, though, and they remained dry inside, although the coolness had them shivering. They had thin blankets to keep them warm, but it wasn't enough.

Florie topped up the bowls and jugs with rain water collected by her pipe system. She boiled the water so they could warm their hands on the bowls.

The sound of the rain and the winds kept them awake for most of the night. When daylight shone through the cracks around the door and windows, the rains and the winds stopped. Even the temperature seemed to rise again.

"It's getting warm," Florie said.

"Yes."

"Evie," Florie said.

"Yes?"

Florie rested her hand on Evie's.

"You shouldn't touch me. I don't know what I will do to you."

"Never mind that, Evie, it will be fine." She stared at Evie, though. Stared until Evie became a little uncomfortable with the scrutiny.

"Are you all right?" Florie asked.

"Yes, why do you ask?"

"You don't seem so good."

"Thanks."

"Seriously, Evie, you look odd, and you're hot, too." She touched Evie's forehead with the back of her hand. "You're really hot. It's no wonder I don't feel the cold so much with you to warm us up."

Evie hugged her knees to her chest. She didn't feel so good, either. She inspected her hands. Thin lines of black, like tiny black veins, spread under her skin.

"I didn't purge," Evie said.

"You were saving it," Florie said.

"And now I'm infected. How did that happen?"

"Purge it now, Evie. Purge it."

Evie crawled from under the blanket. She didn't realise how weak she was until she tried to stand. Her head swam, and her vision blurred. She managed to crawl to the opposite corner of the room and leaned across one of the troughs.

"Come on, quick," Florie said.

"I'm trying to get rid of it," Evie replied.

Nothing happened, no matter how much effort she used. The more she tried to force herself to purge, the worse she felt. Needles of fire spread across her skin, and the illness spread through her body. "I can't do it."

Florie wrapped Evie in all the blankets they had and made her drink warm water.

"I have a little soup. Should I warm it up?"

Evie shook her head. "Save it for later. The water is good."

Over the following hours, her temperature rose as the fever grew. The blackness no longer travelled through her skin; instead, the corruption burrowed deep inside her body and began to infect her organs.

"Well, this is a grand way to learn a lesson," Evie said.

"What lesson are you learning?"

"That I can't hold the sickness."

"Purge it," Florie said.

"I know, I know. I've tried, and I still can't."

Evie had never considered the possibility of sickness before; she had avoided every kind of sickness as a child, and her resistance had continued as an adult. She'd assumed her immunity lay in her Gift, but now it had turned against her.

She lay on her side in the corner. Her whole body hurt. Every breath seemed to rain fire in her chest.

"What now, Evie? Tell me what to do."

"I don't know." She shivered. "I'm cold."

"And hot." Florie added all of the straw around the mattress and the blankets, but it didn't help. Evie shivered so hard, her teeth chattered.

For the second time, Florie had to care for Evie as she lay on her side.

This time, Florie used leftover soup to make a hot weak drink, and not for the first time, Evie thanked her lucky stars that her friend was a fire-starter.

"Are you going to be all right?" Florie asked.

"Yes, I'll sleep it off."

"Can you do that?"

"I hope so, Florie," Evie replied. But she didn't improve at all during the day.

The rain returned, but the storm didn't. They could hear the light rain as it tapped against the roof, and water dripped along the pipes for Florie to collect.

Not much light came through the windows, and such a dull day kept the stables in near darkness.

Evie found a mug with a little cold tea in it. She added more water and swallowed the cool liquid in one go. It tasted wonderful. She helped herself to a little more water and returned to her mat.

Florie stared at her, but Evie ignored her. It took all of her energy just to move that little bit. She lay back on the mat and shivered with the cold at the same time as she burned up. Her sweat-drenched clothing clung to her body and rubbed across her back.

"You've got a fever," Florie said. "Evie, you are really sick."

"I know," Evie said, her teeth chattered.

"Let me help you sit up. I'll get you out of those wet things and make you a hot tea or something."

Evie held up her hand. "Don't touch me, Florie. You might catch something."

"I'm fine. I touched you earlier and nothing happened."

"But an infection can take a long while to show."

"I'll be fine.

"You know what can happen when I'm—"

"Shush," Florie interrupted.

She helped Evie out of her shirt and pulled up her own. She hugged her then, skin to skin.

"No, Florie, what are you doing?" Evie said. She coughed as the phlegm in her throat rose up.

"I'm trying to make you warm or something."

"Don't do this. I can't control myself, and I might do something I'll regret."

"If it helps, then that's fine."

"No."

Florie ignored her protestations and held her closer. "It'll be all right."

Evie could say nothing more because it was already too late. Her body, her Gift, did what it always did, and started to rid itself of the sickness that infected her.

In spite of herself, Evie purged into Florie.

They screamed together.

Evie screamed with the horror of what she had done.

Florie screamed as every drop of corruption surged into her. Tears of pain leaked from the corners of her eyes, and when Evie had done, Florie sank to the floor and curled into a ball.

She breathed, though, and she didn't die. "Florie," Evie

said. Lost for words. She felt better. Normal. Perfect. A little sweaty and clammy, but otherwise just like new.

"It hurts, Evie. It hurts so much."

She looked dreadful. Streamers of black and purple raced under her skin, and if it had been anyone else, Evie might have watched in fascination. She shook her head. "I'm sorry. I don't always have control."

After a few moments, Florie turned over and lay on her back. "Evie, you do have control."

"I don't. How can you say that? There's no way I wanted to pass this on to you."

"I know, but you needed to." She stopped talking as she scrunched her face in a rictus of pain. Her back arched as muscles contracted and pulled her every which way. For a moment, Evie thought she would hurt herself even more.

"Your Gift will always try to keep you alive," she breathed. "Even when you have no wish to, your Gift will keep you safe."

"Safe? I am not so sure. Not anymore."

Florie grimaced. "You're learning, Evie."

Evie stared at Florie, but although she could see the infection burrowing into her, she had no sense of it yet. She could pull at it, as she had with the last man, but she knew, instinctively, that she needed to be more certain here. She ran her hands over Florie's fingers, but even though she called to the sickness, it didn't respond.

"Can you fix this?"

Evie nodded. "I think so. I took a sickness I'd passed on out of Bethwood, so I should be able to do the same for you. I need to watch it settle."

"Okay," Florie whispered. Her voice had softened, as though the sickness raked at her throat and chest.

"Stay with me, Florie. I can't yet see it."

Florie stared at Evie.

"You say I'm learning. What have I learned so far?"

"Tell me."

"The first lesson is that I can hold the sickness, but not for long."

Florie nodded.

"The second lesson is that in times of need, I don't get to choose what happens. My Gift does the choosing, and it will do what it will to survive."

Florie clenched her teeth as though biting back pain.

"I also know I can pass it on. Sometimes I can choose to release, as I did with Eric. Sometimes it is like a reflex, as it was with Bethwood and you."

"Yes," Florie hissed. Her pale skin had lost the tendrils of black; they'd sunk into her, but her skin had flushed with the signs of fever.

"Now, I will see if I can heal you." Evie stared at Florie and cleared her mind of all extraneous thoughts.

She did not have time to worry about what would or would not work, she needed her Gift to do what it did. She pulled at Florie's shirt and exposed the pale skin of her chest and torso. There were many old injuries mapped out on her young skin. A long and ragged cut that had healed in a bumpy line. A burn scar along the edge of her ribs; one bruise, not too old either, ran across her sides and over her hip.

"You've been marked," Evie said.

"The hazards of a fire-starter in Bristelle," she answered.

"I will not let you go," Evie said.

"I know."

Then she saw it. The sickness.

No longer under the skin, it burrowed deep within Florie's body. It stood out like a shadow and Evie could see it as shadow and blood. Like fingers, the shadows reached out and started to spread through her lungs. Tendrils of black multiplied through her chest and prepared to strangle her heart. Evie knew that if this didn't work, Florie would die soon. It had become so virulent, so aggressive, that she didn't have time to waste.

"I'm too weak," she said. "I might not be able to do this."

"It's all right, Evie."

Evie howled, "No, it isn't." She touched Florie's skin and called to the sickness with the desperation of one who dared not fail. The infection readily responded to her touch. Yet she pulled out not even a half of it before she could do no more. Florie, however, breathed better, her skin lost its flush, and her temperature seemed to stabilise somewhere near normal.

Evie leaned over the slop bucket and purged. Black oil, sticky and stinky, splodged into the half full bucket like thick greasy oil. It was an unpleasant thing to do, but necessary. Evie leaned against the wall, exhausted.

"You need energy," Florie croaked.

"Yes."

"We have fruitcake remember. Eat it. Don't let yourself sicken again."

Evie wasted no time; she took a bite of the heavy fruit-filled confection, chewed fast, and swilled it down with cold water. The taste of the purge filled her mouth and spoiled the flavour of the food. Yet she bit, chewed, and swallowed. Over and over.

She could feel her energy return as she ate. More than the sweetness, now she needed something more savoury.

"Meat pie, too, if you need." It was almost as though Florie had read her mind.

Evie ate that, too, and waited a few minutes more for the goodness of the food to fill her. She knelt by Florie's side. Evie focussed her thoughts on Florie and the darkness. "Come to me," she said. As though she could make the illness do her bidding.

"Don't be daft, talking to it," Florie said.

"It will respond," Evie said, and she placed her hand upon Florie's bare chest.

The moment she did, the blackness responded. She called to it. Not with words, talking made her feel awkward, but she called with her thoughts and her will. She called, and it came to her. Almost every last drop of it.

She knew that some of it remained behind, like a dirty part of herself. However weakened it might be, Florie had not been cured.

Evie purged into the slop bucket again and made sure she was empty.

"That's better," Florie said.

Evie examined Florie as best she could. Her cheeks were pink and healthy, her skin smooth and without obvious blemish. For this, Evie considered herself lucky. It could have been so much worse. Florie wasn't strong enough for a sickness like this. She would need to wait for the two of them to be more resilient and hope that she could put right the wrong she had done.

"There is another lesson here, Florie. Once taken, a disease seems to grow faster and with more vigour than the original. It is almost as though I fed it and concentrated the essence into something far greater."

"You have, Evie."

"I am what Godwyn wanted. A weapon of great power. I can't allow this to continue."

"You must, Evie. Make it a good power." Florie coughed then. Wracking coughs that made her fold over.

"I need you to be well, Florie," Evie said. "Stay with me."

Evie wrapped her in one of the blankets and helped her onto the mattress in the far corner that had fewer drafts to worry about. This time, Evie would be the one to take care of Florie.

She had learned another lesson, too. Now she knew that no matter how virulent the sickness, she could grab it with no ill effect, so long as she did it in a timely fashion.

She waited Florie slept in a comfortable manner, and then

she joined her. For now, she'd had enough of lessons. She curled up with Florie, and, completely exhausted, soon fell asleep.

W hen Bethwood came to visit. He took one look at them drenched in sweat and backed out of the shed again. He covered his nose.

"It stinks in here. What the hell is going on?"

Evie couldn't smell anything, but they had both been sick, so the pollution, illness, and sweat probably whiffed quite bad. Besides, Evie knew she didn't ooze rose water when she worked her Gift.

"More water," Evie croaked.

"Are you…"

"Fine. We're sick. It will go," Evie said. "Need soup to fight infection." It was a cheek, but they were in desperate need of more nourishment. "Soup, meat, sweet tea, fruitcake." If they needed to get better, she might as well ask for all she could get away with.

Bethwood backed out of the shed and locked them in again. He didn't say anything, and Evie wondered if he'd leave them there.

Her answer came a little later that day. One of the guards opened the door and threw a pile of clothing and an extra blanket into the stables. He slid a tray along the floor, too.

Evie could smell the soup. That wasn't all. He'd added hot tea, and when she took a sip, it was sweetened. The bread was not so stale; it would last if they hoarded some of it. He'd added a small square of fruitcake and a thick slice of cheese. They were being spoiled.

"Florie," Evie said, and gave her a good shake.

"What?"

"Food. You need to eat to regain your strength."

She grunted and sat up. "Yes, I know."

"Do you feel like eating?" Evie asked.

Florie's stomach grumbled.

"We'll have soup then, and save the rest for later."

Florie, always the optimistic one, remained quiet throughout their meal. Once she'd finished, she said, "I almost died, didn't I, Evie?"

For a moment, Evie didn't know what to say. In the end, the truth had to be said. "Yes, almost."

"Just like Eric, then."

"Not quite. You're stronger than he was."

"Do you think being Gifted helps?"

Evie shrugged. "I don't know. Perhaps. There's something else, Florie."

"Like what?"

"I'm not sure I cleared everything out. So if you ever feel sick, tell me."

"I will." Florie wrapped her arms around her. "I'm tired now."

"You need sleep. We both need sleep."

"Will you hold me?" Florie asked.

"I'm not sure that's a good idea."

"You purged, though, didn't you?"

Evie nodded.

"Then you can't infect me again, can you? Don't argue with me, I'm right, I know I am."

Evie smiled at her. "If you say so." But she wasn't sure if she was right and that worried her. What if she took the remaining illness from Florie, kept it long enough to make it worse, and gave it back to her?

Florie seemed to read her mind. "It'll be all right. We're safe now."

Evie wished she could be as sure. Yet she relented, and as they curled up together, both of them soon fell asleep. They slept all the way through the night and didn't wake until well into the morning. Even then, they only awoke because Evie jumped at the sound of the doors being flung open.

A guard shoved a tray inside the pen, took the old slop bucket, and replaced it with an empty one.

"You stink," he said, and slammed the doors closed and locked them in again.

Florie stretched. "What do we have this time?"

Evie fetched the tray. "Two generous bowls of thin porridge with a touch of honey."

"Ohh, nice," Florie said, she already sounded like her usual self.

"Hungry?"

"Starved."

Evie handed her a bowl and grabbed the spoons they'd been given before. She didn't feel at all hungry, though. If anything, the smell turned her stomach. Florie ate all of hers and half of Evie's.

"It's good," she said, and smacked her lips together. "You should eat."

"I'm not hungry."

"You need your strength."

"Too much cheese, I think."

Florie nodded. "Let's not overdo the feast tonight, then."

Evie chuckled. There was nothing she could add to that.

11

The weeks passed by in a steady routine. Bethwood took them out most days, and they saw a variety of people who needed to be made well. All of them were rich or important. Most of them ignored her outright, some were pompous, and some were polite but dismissive. Evie didn't care.

She met lots of important and influential people. Some of them were titled and important simply because they had an important father. Many of the people she met were professionals: medics, a magistrate, a surgeon, a tutor at the university, and several men of the legal profession. Evie even used her skill on a senior nurse at the hospital who was as full of self-importance as some of those with titles.

On the whole, the sicknesses she removed were more of the same old same old. Men, she decided, needed to be a little more careful of where they shoved their privates. She couldn't remember any of their names, if she'd been given them at all. Except for the nurse, but that was a whole different thing.

Evie retained the sickness after every visit, and afterwards she went to the prisons where she unloaded. The prisoners, she remembered. Marley Pertman the Slasher, John Smith the Poisoner. John Harris, Goff Layman, and Vaugh Darren were all guilty of various forms of abuse, often against young people. Bethwood knew how to anger Evie, and sometimes they took Florie into the prison so he could impress upon Evie the transience of the younger woman's existence and how it depended upon his goodwill.

Of all of them, Zacharia Jedicus was a name Evie could never forget. Bethwood had chosen the man with great care. Unlike the other inmates awaiting the gallows, this one had a cell to himself, with food, water, and a slop bucket. He wore clean clothes and had with him a book. Not only could he read, he could afford to do it in prison. Evie knew this man was someone e special.

"This is Zacharia Jedicus," Bethwood announced when they were in his cell.

He was a tall, reed thin chap, clean shaven, and wore a suit. A suit in prison.

The man rose to his feet. "And you are?" he asked in a deep, rich voice.

Bethwood pulled back his shoulders. "My name is Godwyn Bethwood, and this little stripling is Evie Chester."

"And the reason for your visit is?"

"I'll get to that. In a moment," Bethwood answered. He turned to Evie. "This man calls himself an agent of God who must purify the world of the 'filth of the Gifted,' as he calls it."

The man nodded.

"The filth of the Gifted," Evie said.

"He discovered twenty-five—" Bethwood started.

"Twenty-seven," Jedicus corrected.

"My apologies, twenty-seven Gifted as a part of his mission in life. What did you do to these twenty-seven people?"

"They are not people, Mr Bethwood. They are a filth that must be eradicated before they infect the whole world."

Evie glared at him. "I see. And you killed them when you found them?"

Jedicus sighed. "No. To rid the world of them, we must understand what makes these verminous creature as they are. These Gifted were found and used as experiments for surgeons and those like me, those who understand the workings of the world in finer and greater detail."

"You experimented on them?" Evie asked.

"Indeed we did. Repeatedly and extensively." He sounded proud of himself, and Evie grew angrier by the minute.

"I bet it was a painful set of experiments, too," she said.

He nodded. "We did what needed to be done to understand them. Taking them apart was the first stage."

"They are people, Mr Jedicus, not machines to be disassembled and remade," Evie said.

"Of course they are not machines. Machines have a use. Neither are they real people, even if they have the appearance of such. Once taken apart, we had no desire to put any of them back together." He laughed at his own wit.

Evie found herself boiling inside. "In that case, Jedicus, I have a proposal for you."

He glared at her. "And what, pray tell, can a stripling like you have to offer me in the way of a proposal?"

Evie glanced at Bethwood.

Bethwood shrugged. "Up to you, Evie. This is your experiment, after all."

"What do you mean?" Jedicus asked. His eyes narrowed with suspicion. "I think you should leave now."

Bethwood stood in front of Jedicus and pushed him backwards until he had to sit on his stone sleeping shelf. "Not yet, Jedicus. Evie hasn't finished with you. In fact, she hasn't started yet. But you know, I think this is going to hurt. Or maybe not." He shrugged. "What do you think, Evie?"

Evie pulled up her sleeves. "I think I can learn a great deal here today. I'm almost full, and I have no place to be."

Bethwood grinned. "Let's see what you have in mind. Mr Zachary Jedicus is going nowhere either. He is, if you like, a captive audience."

"I know what she is, and you can't do this," Jedicus blustered.

"Well now, you see, I can," Bethwood said. "Everyone has a price, and I can assure you I have paid above the odds to gain access to a person like you."

Evie stepped closer and touched the back of Jedicus' hand with the tip of her finger. He flinched at her touch.

"Don't dawdle, girl," Bethwood instructed.

"Yes, sir," she said. She reached out and grabbed Jedicus' hand. "Please don't struggle," she told him.

Evie unloaded into him with such thoughtful and controlled slowness that she didn't even detect the disease under his skin. Neither did Jedicus, which made her think this slow delivery could be pain free should she wish it.

"Done?" Bethwood asked. He sounded disappointed.

"Yes, but that was too easy," Evie said. She called to the sickness in Jedicus and collected it back into herself.

"Let's try it this way," she said. She considered the sickness, and although she wondered if she could actively increase the potency, she didn't have the time to test her theory. Instead, she opted to unload in quick and certain bursts.

Every time she did, Jedicus screamed.

"Good girl, Evie," Bethwood said.

Once done, she wiped her hand on her skirt. "Mr Jedicus, thank you for your patience. I hope they hang you soon."

"Filth," he responded.

"Perhaps, but I get to leave this place, and you do not. And I can tell you this—the longer they wait, the sicker you will become." She stared at him for a moment, and she saw where the sickness had started to accumulate in his body. "Tomorrow, you will piss blood. Within a week, you'll be shitting your innards out every time you move. You won't die quick, though. Instead, this will become something increasingly unpleasant for every one of your last days."

"You are no better than the others," Jedicus said.

Evie snorted. "There is one thing for you to consider. I may not have much, but I have hope, and more importantly, I'll not be pissing blood every day."

She turned to Bethwood.

"Done?" Bethwood asked. He grinned at her. He'd enjoyed the entire exchange.

"Yes, let's leave him to rot. A cup of tea in fresh air, away from the stench of this rotten egg, would be lovely."

Bethwood laughed.

If Evie had any regrets, it was that she never saw the results of her abilities. She never knew if the healed ones appreciated her skill, or what life they led afterwards. She never knew the effects of the infections and corruptions she unloaded into the condemned men either. Her promises as to how things would progress were little more than guesses.

She did notice a few things. She wasn't a passive sponge soaking up illness. She had become something more. She could see infections and corruption when she wished it. Not all the time, but even that was helpful.

12

_____

One Sunday afternoon, Bethwood collected them and ushered them into his open carriage. Evie and Florie sat opposite him. Wiggins sat up top with the groom, and Evie could hear him grumble pretty much every step of the way.

Given a choice, Evie would have preferred Grobber to be with them. He was mean, but Wiggins wasn't just a bully, he'd shown himself to be the sort to take malicious nastiness to a whole new level. He liked to try and get away with all kinds of sneaky spitefulness because he knew they would not fight back. They couldn't. The consequences would be far worse.

As Evie considered all the things she might do to Wiggins, the coach stopped in the middle of Bristelle. "Where are we?" she asked as she stared up at the portico to a huge building on Phipps Street.

"Are you taking us to the theatre, Mr Bethwood?" Florie asked.

It looked deserted. Two pairs of heavy wooden doors closed the entrance off.

Bethwood pulled out his pocket watch and, after he had

checked the time, stared at Florie. "You should not speak out of turn, fire-starter. You have little use here. Little use in general, in fact."

"Sorry," Florie said. She turned her gaze down and stared at the floor.

"It would be nice to know why we are here, Mr Bethwood," Evie said.

He nodded to himself, put the watch back, and opened the carriage door. "Side road," he yelled to the driver. "That way."

When he sat down, he stared at Evie. "We are going to see someone special, and she means a great deal to me."

"And you wish me to heal her?"

"Yes."

"Do you wish me to leave some behind?"

He shook his head. "No, Evie, cure her. Totally and absolutely. I want no doubt."

This was the first time he'd asked her to heal anyone since Eric. Something had happened, or would happen. "I will do what I can, Mr Bethwood."

"Good, because this is important," he said. He smiled as he spoke and stared at Evie. "Very important."

Important?

Evie had no prescience or mind-reading abilities, she couldn't tell truth from lies, or fact from fiction. What she did know was when things felt different, and right now, everything felt different.

"Everything we have done so far has been in preparation for this moment, hasn't it?" she asked.

"Don't be cheeky," he answered. "You are correct, however."

"What is the sickness?"

"Listen, Evie, this is not like any other sickness. This is very different, and I could find no other instances of an illness of this nature for you to practice with."

"What about all the medics?"

"We have seen every medic and healer in the city and beyond. No one can help us."

"What about the Healing Towers of Knaresville? I hear they're the best."

"They are, but they can't do anything for her," Bethwood said.

"And you think I can? I am no healer."

"No one can do what you do, Evie, and not in the way that you do it."

"I rip sickness from people."

"That is what I need you to do here. Whatever it takes. Rip it out and make her well."

Evie's mind whirred. Bethwood needed this more than anything he had asked of her before. That had been business, pure and simple. This was different. Different gave her some power.

"What if I can't?" she asked.

He stared at her and thought through his answer. "This will be your last client," he answered. His tone chilled her to the bone.

Evie didn't want to ask what he meant. "In that case, I need to know what I'm looking for. You need to give me a chance to think about how to do it. I need to consider all the reasons why the other healers couldn't help."

"You never needed to know so much before."

"That was different. Most times, the sickness has more to do with where those men go seeking their fun."

He nodded. "It doesn't matter, Evie. This is different in every way it could be different. You'll know plenty soon enough."

The carriage clattered along a dirty alley that ran adjacent to the theatre and to the rear of the building. All the buildings around the alley stood three or four storeys high, and little light reached the ground. External stairs crawled along the rear of one building, and when Evie looked up, she saw amongst the rails and the washing lines filled with drying clothing small faces watching what they did.

At the rear end of the building, she saw a set of black-painted doors. Bethwood got out of the coach and banged on the door with the end of his walking stick. *Boom, boom, boom.* Three times.

It took a while for anyone to answer, but eventually the door opened, and a chap in work clothes stepped outside. It wasn't the clothing that drew Evie's attention, it was the moustache. It covered his face and drooped down like a hairy scarf. She had never seen such a thing. When he smiled, the whole moustache bounced up and smiled with him. She couldn't help herself, she stared at him.

"Hello, Mr Bethwood, how are you this fine day?"

"Fine, fine," he answered.

"Come in. You know the way," Mr Moustache said. He had a broad accent that made his words slur together, punctuated with over-pronounced consonants.

"Thank you, Ravanich. Why is the front not open?"

"A new programme, Mr Bethwood. A late start today."

"Oh, of course. But I thought that was a week away?"

"Supposed to be, but between you and me, the last one didn't do so well, so management wants the new show ready as soon as. Rehearsals have started, and we've been at it all day. We'll put on the old show tonight, and the matinee will be for the new form."

"Ahh, understandable. Does that not become hard to remember?"

Ravanich nodded. "Sometimes. But we are professionals, and we can do anything." He waved his hands about and bowed in a most extravagant and showy fashion. "Come on in."

Bethwood turned to the two women behind him. "Come on, girls, don't dawdle. Get yourselves inside."

"Both of us?" Florie asked.

"Yes, girl. Now hurry up. Haven't got all day." He held the door open as they jumped down onto the cobbled street. "Mr Wiggins, please stay with the carriage and make sure no one nicks anything."

Wiggins didn't look too happy at being left outside. Maybe he wanted to go into the theatre, too.

Once inside, the door slammed shut, and they were cast into a twilit world where all illumination came from lamps, and it was not much light at that. Even in the half light, Evie could still see details. The walls were covered in grand and colourful posters. A bright and gaudy world she would never have hoped to explore.

"Girls, please, we will take all day if you stare at each picture," he said. But Evie detected no harshness in his voice. If anything, their reactions amused him.

She took one last look at a poster and grabbed Florie's hand. "Come on, time to move. With luck, we can see more of this later."

"Evie, we're in a theatre!" Florie said. Her excitement made her voice rise.

"Wait until you see the stage," Bethwood said.

"Can I?" Florie asked.

"We're going to go right by," he answered. He grinned as he spoke. Evie could hardly believe this was the same man who'd locked them in an outbuilding and forced them to do his bidding.

Even so, Florie gawped at every picture, her mouth open as she caught sight of so many. Not just over all the beautiful men and women, but the costumes and flamboyance of it all.

They strode along the corridor, and it was a different world. One filled with a whole range of novel perceptions and experiences. There were people smells. Perspiration, grease, flowers dried and fresh, rose water and other aromatics assaulted Evie's nose. She could smell food, too, and her stomach rumbled.

The noise, however, took some getting used to.

People raced by, and when they spoke, they seemed unable to speak at a normal volume. Loud and excited, their voices turned to shouts, yet not in anger. Laughter, too, blossomed from unexpected places and billowed out in good cheer.

The light did not increase in the passageways they followed. There were no windows here and only a few gas lamps, all turned to a minimal glow.

They passed an open doorway where bright light spilled out into the dark corridor. When Evie looked inside, she saw a dozen people all squashed into a tiny room. Men and women, all in various stages of undress as they vied for the single mirror and the light. They applied bright colours to their skin and sang songs for the joy of singing.

Florie, distracted by it all, walked into a wall.

"Look to it," Bethwood said. "Watch where you're going." He seemed amused, though, and that was always a good sign. An unexpected and odd sign, but welcome nonetheless.

"What's going on there?" Evie asked.

"They're getting ready to perform," Bethwood answered.

"Can we watch them?" Florie asked.

"Later," he said. That, too, was not like the Bethwood they knew.

They stepped with care along the sides of the auditorium, a grand room with columns and seats everywhere. The walls held balconies, and although they were in darkness, Evie could see the seats there, too. Red velvet seats with gold trim, and they shone. Colours burst from the walls in shades of gold and silver, reds, yellows, and a blue so bright it hurt her eyes.

Young men and women bustled about as they carried set pieces from the wings onto the stage. In front of the stage, in a sunken area, musicians wandered about and practiced their music. They didn't all practice the same music, nor did they all play at the same time. Rather, they filled the room with a cacophony of sound that drowned out all but the loudest of shouts.

"Come, come," Bethwood said. He guided them backstage into a narrow corridor even darker than the other passages. Steps led upwards, and with the confidence of a known route, he led them up the stairs to the third floor. He stopped before a black-painted door with a handle that shone like polished gold. He didn't wait to be invited inside. He turned the handle and opened the door as though he had all the right in the world.

Bethwood took a step across the threshold and held the door open so Evie could see inside. Her eyes skirted over the details of the room. Plush, well-appointed, and large, with a small fireplace in the corner and a large window over the street. An open door led off to one side where she could see the edge of a metal-framed bed. An open wardrobe displayed more clothing than she had ever seen in one place. Her attention skimmed over these details and focused on the occupant of the room.

Bethwood cleared his throat. "Hello, Hesta, how are you? I have brought company."

Evie turned her attention to the woman who sat in the wingback chair in front of the fire. She wore a long satin gown, the rich olive-green fabric edged with fine stitchwork. She wore a cream shawl draped over her shoulders and wrapped around her neck. In one hand she held a crystal goblet, and her other hand draped over the armrest of the chair.

Evie's first thoughts, as she took in the view of the woman, was that she was so beautiful she hurt the eyes. Her features were so fine that, if anything, she appeared fragile, almost ethereal. Evie felt large and base just standing there.

Her skin, a light brown, shone in the light from the open window and contrasted with her hair, a brown so dark it glowed almost as much as her eyes.

The woman, Hesta, put down her glass. Her gaze flew from Evie, to Florie, and then to Bethwood. She nodded once, and her hands became a flurry of activity.

"Yes, I know, but I said I would come," Bethwood said out of the blue.

She responded with more gestures.

Bethwood gave up speaking and moved his hands in a series of shapes and forms that Evie could neither follow nor understand.

Hesta rose to her feet and stood with her hands on her hips as she stared at Bethwood.

"Don't look at me like that," he said. His hand gestures were a little slower now, almost half-hearted.

Hesta, however, was not done with him. Her hands gained momentum, and they moved so fast Evie swore they left a trail of sparks behind.

"All right," Bethwood said.

She smiled, and when they stopped their gesturing, she stepped close to Bethwood and hugged him. Like old friends.

She tapped Bethwood's arm, caught his attention, and gesticulated with one hand and a shrug of the shoulders.

"Yes, this is she," Bethwood said.

More hand signs came from both of them, and Evie got the impression that Bethwood spoke for their benefit, not Hesta's.

"Yes, I know I should have called first and warned you, but—"

Hesta grabbed Bethwood's arm and shook him so that he stopped talking. He nodded and put his hand on Evie's shoulder. "This is Evie Chester. And the other one is Florie."

Evie found herself under the intense scrutiny of the woman who did not speak.

When Bethwood began to speak, she held up a hand. Surprisingly, he held his words and said no more.

Who was this woman, Evie thought, who could silence a man like Bethwood with nothing more than a wave of her fingers?

Hesta reached out as though to touch Evie's face, but instead she stayed her hand. She turned to Bethwood, and they resumed their dance of hand and fingers.

"But I said I would," he said.

She nodded.

"Will you let her heal you?" Bethwood sounded most hesitant.

Hesta's fingers and hands powered through a series of gestures.

"I know you're not sick!" Bethwood said. "But she could make a difference."

"Do you need my help?" Evie asked.

"Let her," he said. He gestured with his fingers.

The woman wiggled her fingers back.

"Don't be rude. Evie is here to help you."

She frowned and stood with her hands on her hips again, as though she were some high and mighty lord ready to lay down the law. Annoyance marred her features for all of a heartbeat or two, and then she smiled.

That was all the encouragement he needed. "I would love to hear you sing again."

She shook her head in exasperation and started to gesture with her hands. This time she grew so animated, she banged her own chest hard enough to make a thud.

Bethwood turned his eyes to the floor. "I know. I'm sorry, but what could I do? I had to do something."

Hesta strode around Bethwood and opened the door. She patted him on the arm until he looked at her, then gestured outside. With a slump of his shoulders, he left the room. "Come, Florie, we will wait outside," he said.

Evie started to follow them, but Bethwood shook his head. "Do as you are told and do the best you can," he said. "And remember what I told you."

Evie stood frozen in the middle of the room. Did he mean the instructions in the coach, or his general instructions? She did not need reminding of any threats to herself or Florie.

Hesta ignored her for a moment, her attention focussed on Florie and Bethwood as they walked down the hall and down the stairs.

"You want me to stay?" Evie asked.

Hesta closed the door. She pointed at a stool and waited for Evie to sit.

"I'm sorry, I think you speak with your hands, and I have no idea what all that means. Tell me where it hurts, and I will see what I can do."

Hesta waved off Evie's words and sat back in her own seat. She raised a finger to her lips and regarded Evie with careful and intense scrutiny.

Embarrassed, Evie focussed on the olive-coloured damask upholstery of Hesta's chair. It almost matched her dress.

The sound of Hesta drumming her fingers on the padded armrest drew Evie's attention upward. She settled her attention on Hesta's hands as if they would move and she would be able to understand this hand-speaking they did.

After a while, when nothing happened, Evie let her gaze rise towards Hesta's face. Hesta stared back for a moment, and Evie wasn't sure how she was supposed to react.

Hesta waved her hands to gain Evie's attention. She pointed to Evie and then to herself.

"Do you want me to examine you? I can't understand this hand speaking."

Hesta smiled, but she nodded.

"All right, then."

Hesta unwrapped her scarf from her shoulders, but she stopped halfway.

"Do you need help?"

Hesta shook her head and gritted her teeth. She closed her eyes for a moment, and then she ripped off the shawl to expose the extensive damage to her neck and throat.

Evie gasped when she saw the ravaged skin. Lined and burned, her neck bore the imprint of a hand as it melted through her skin. "Oh, goodness me!" she exclaimed, and looked away.

Hesta sat still and said nothing.

"Does Bethwood know what this is?" Evie asked.

Hesta nodded.

"He knows what I can do, and he knows I am no healer. Oh, goodness, miss Bethwood, you need to see a proper healer. Not me. I'm insufficient for this."

Evie stared at her hands as her thoughts ran wild. No matter what, this poor woman needed help. What on earth was Bethwood thinking?

Her thoughts were interrupted when Hesta moved to kneel in front of her. She reached out to touch her face. She pointed at Evie and to her neck.

"You want me to... to what? Do something?"

Hesta nodded.

"You know, I wish I could heal you, but this is not the sort of thing I generally encounter. I deal with sickness, not scars and inflammations. Bethwood should have informed you better."

Hesta patted Evie's knees and frowned. She shook her head, and if Evie thought of anything, she thought Hesta seemed irritated with her.

Evie tried to smile, but she couldn't. Instead, Hesta reached out for her hands.

"No," Evie said.

Hesta cocked her head to one side and quirked an eyebrow.

"It always hurts people when they touch me."

For a moment, Evie could have sworn Hesta tried to smile, but she held it. Instead, she gripped one of Evie's hands in both of hers and guided it to the destruction visited upon her neck.

Her fingers touched Hesta's ravaged skin even though she didn't want to make contact. The poor woman had suffered enough without her adding to it.

Hesta did not let her hand go, and Evie's fingers slipped around Hesta's throat. Hesta stared into her eyes as though she would see the answer there.

Evie expected to feel the ragged scarring of the burns, and she did feel that first. Then she felt something different. A darkness of sorts, unlike any infection she had ever seen or felt. The heat of an infection that wasn't really an infection.

"This is different," Evie said. She concentrated on the sensations under her fingers and the call of her Gift that touched Hesta. There was something that seemed familiar and yet strange and unknown.

At that moment, it didn't occur to her to wonder how they could be in physical contact without the infection that wrapped her throat responding to her touch.

Hesta reached out and touched the side of Evie's head.

"I know, I know. I'm trying, but it's so different."

Hesta smiled. She tapped Evie in the middle of her forehead and leaned forward until their heads touched. As they contacted skin to skin, an explosion of colour and sound inside Evie's thoughts almost took her breath away.

'Hello, Evie Chester. My name is Hesta Estrallia, and we have a great deal in common,' she said without her voice, but straight into her mind.

Evie leaned away. "What the hell was that?"

Hesta reached out and prodded Evie in the middle of her forehead. *'Me,'* she said telepathically.

"What the fuck!"

Hesta pressed her cool, almost cold, hands against Evie's

cheeks and cupped her face. Evie couldn't look away, and she couldn't escape. Hesta's brown eyes stared into Evie's own, and for a moment, she felt exposed and open to that intense gaze.

'Not all Gifts are the same,' Hesta said inside her mind.

Evie swallowed the lump in her throat and blinked. "I don't know what to say."

'Some Gifts are more useful than others, and mine just terrifies everyone. If you are Gifted and scared, what use is this to an ordinary and mundane person?'

"Can you speak to Bethwood like this?"

'Godwyn never listens.'

"But you can talk into my mind?"

'Yes.'

"Do we have to touch?"

Hesta shook her head. *'Now that we have touched, so long as I can see you, I can speak to you like this.'*

"Can I do it?"

'Try.'

Evie grinned. *'What a brilliant skill for thieves.'* Her thoughts transmitted to Hesta without a hitch.

'Evie!'

"Shall I examine your neck now? Any more surprises?"

'You tell me.'

Evie closed her eyes and explored Hesta's neck with both hands. Smooth skin surrounded the giant handprint. "You know, I *can* sense something," she said.

'Concentrate.'

Evie's mind sharpened, focussed with single-minded clarity, until her only thoughts revolved around Hesta. Beautiful Hesta with the ruined neck that had been ravaged by…

Her eyes flew open. "This is no disease or sickness."

Hesta stared at Evie and shook her head.

Evie resumed her scrutiny of the burned area. Skin,

hardened and ridged by damage. White scars, pink scars, and blazing red and purple infection warred across Hesta's neck. "There are old scars, and some of this appears fresh and newly made."

Hesta nodded.

"And the scarring is still forming?"

She nodded again, but more vigorously.

With gentle fingertips, Evie explored the feel of this skin that looked as though it had melted and set. "This must have hurt. I can only guess at the pain."

Hesta closed her eyes and took a deep breath, her nod almost imperceptible.

To Evie's careful touch, the ordinary skin felt smooth and cool. She lingered over the soft skin before again touching the ravaged parts. When she did, heat burned through her fingers as though a furnace lay within. She gripped Hesta's throat in one hand, her hand not quite big enough to cover the mutilation, and the similarity between her grip and the marks on Hesta's skin could not be ignored.

"It is not sickness," Evie repeated. "This is like magic. An enchantment. A curse."

She closed her eyes and opened herself. The infection, although she couldn't really call it an infection, came to her then in tentative but searing streams of wrongness.

"Not a sickness, not an infection, but a curse." Evie smiled as understanding came to her. It didn't behave like a sickness, either. Tendrils of the curse had wrapped around Hesta's neck like iron bands that marked the skin and burrowed deep into her throat. Evie had to unwrap each one with care. "I wish I'd had medical training. I bet this would be a lot easier to understand."

Hesta cocked her head to one side and smiled.

Evie smiled back. "Focus," she reminded herself.

She followed the traces of the curse far into Hesta's flesh and bone. It tried to wriggle away from her, as though it were alive, wanting to stay locked inside. In the end, Evie proved to have the stronger will, and she finally pulled out the last of the corruption. She didn't think that she could do anything for the scarring, but she could stop the curse, if that was what it was.

When she gathered the strands of the curse and unlinked them from Hesta, they raced into Evie. And seared through every inch of her body. It was unlike calling any sickness she had encountered.

"I have it," she said. She looked at her hands and expected to see something different. Sickness acted in one way; she'd never handled a curse. But her hands were normal. No sign of anything. If anything, she thought that odd, or at least unusual.

'Are you all right?' Hesta asked inside her head.

"You do know it's rude messing inside someone head? Can you see what I am thinking?"

Hesta shook her head. *'No.'*

She guided Evie to a small wash bowl on a delicate stand in the corner, and Evie prepared to purge. She stopped for a moment to think if Bethwood had given any instructions about this. "How do you know what I need?" she asked.

Hesta coughed. It was a delicate sound, and unexpected.

"It's all right, Evie. Let it out," Hesta said. Her voice sounded a little dry, almost a croak, as though rusty from lack of use.

Evie stiffened and turned to Hesta. "You can speak?"

"It won't last long." Her voice sounded surer, albeit wistful, as though she were rediscovering how to use it. "It never does." In those few words, Evie heard a world of sadness, and she felt sorry for her.

Evie turned back to the washstand, and her thoughts raced.

Hesta seemed to read her thoughts. "Do you need to… What do you call it? I think Godwyn called it a purge?"

"Godwyn Bethwood has spoken of this?"

"Yes, he has spoken of everything."

"I see."

"Now, be a love and do what you need to do. I don't need you succumbing to this, too." She stared into Evie's eyes. "Please, don't sicken. Don't be a victim as well. I couldn't bear it."

Evie didn't need to be asked twice. Given all the sicknesses she'd been exposed to of late, she didn't want to keep this strange affliction inside her any longer than necessary. Especially since whatever it was that affected Hesta could not be considered natural.

With that in mind, Evie closed her eyes and called her Gift. This time, she expected it all to feel different. She could almost feel her power rolling through her, collecting the darkness and herding it through to her hands.

It collected in her fingers first and could best be described as coal tar, black and thick enough to be almost solid. It was a nasty thought to think of it as being inside her. It collected in both of her hands, and she could feel it welling up at the back of her throat.

"Oh, bugger!" Hesta said. "Stop."

Evie faced her, a partial purge in motion, but she didn't call it back.

"I can see it in your hands and your eyes. Your beautiful eyes are starting to turn. Don't. Don't let it go near your eyes. Or anywhere else for that matter."

"I—"

"Don't let it control you, Evie," Hesta said. "You must control it. Send it to one place, all of it. It will only damage your eyes and face if you allow it to leak there."

She turned away from Hesta and faced the washing bowl. She concentrated on her hands, and her fingers turned black and purple. Green pus collected under her fingernails, and she grimaced at the pain of this vileness bursting to escape her body.

Hesta started to rub her hands over Evie's back. "Steady," she said.

For a moment, Evie couldn't move. She took comfort in the touch of another person who had no fear of her. More than that, she wasn't afraid of Hesta either, and that thought distracted her.

The blackness inside stopped seeking a way out and seemed to stay still and undirected. She didn't think about that. All she could think about was warm hands, not touching her skin, but so close, the gesture of familiarity such a rare thing. No one touched her, and she didn't touch them either. She recalled what had happened with Florie and stiffened.

"It's all right, Evie. Focus your mind on what you need to do. Call it to your hands and let it go."

She closed her eyes and turned her thoughts away from Hesta's pleasing, but very distracting, contact.

"Don't hold it back," Hesta advised. She started to hum, and it was as though Evie couldn't stop herself from relaxing.

She visualised her hands more clearly now, and the holes, tiny little holes, appeared in her skin at the sides of her nails. As the skin opened, the pressure lessened and the pain, too. The blackness oozed out a few drops at a time. Then faster as her body rushed to get rid of it. It hurt, though, as the bubbling corruption burst through her skin, more than any other purge she'd done, and she screamed, screamed until her throat ached. All the way through, Hesta rubbed her back and hummed to her.

Once done, she used a little water from the jug to wipe her hands and her face. Her fingers started to heal almost as soon as she had finished. No matter the damage, they seemed to heal far faster than they should have. A small mercy as far as Evie was concerned.

"Is that the best way to cleanse yourself?" Hesta asked.

"It's the only way I know."

Hesta took a glass from the side and added water. "Here, drink," she said. "When Godwyn rushes through the door demanding blood, don't panic. I'll explain how we are safe and sound, and he'll be distracted because I can speak again. Then you and I need to have a little chat about all of this."

13

———————

Evie sat on the stool and stared forward. She did not fear Bethwood because one word from Hesta and he would forget all about her, of that she was reasonably sure. There were other thoughts that danced through her mind.

"How are you feeling?" Hesta asked.

For the first time since Evie had entered the theatre, she reminded herself of who she was and why she was here. A slave, and property of Godwyn Bethwood, she was here to do a job. She had done it well, too.

"You are a quiet one, aren't you?" Hesta said.

"It increases the chance of survival," Evie answered. She fixed her gaze on a spot of rug two inches to the side of Hesta's feet. "And I think I did my job well today."

"Is that all you have to say?"

"It is not my place to comment now that I have done my job."

"Consider this your opportunity to speak, then."

Evie coughed to clear her throat and looked up.

'Talk to me, please.' Hesta said in to her thoughts.

"You know that's rude."

Hesta laughed. It sounded sweet and light, like bells and happiness.

"Who are you? What are you? And what did you do to me?" Evie asked.

Hesta took a drink of water before she answered. "I have already introduced myself."

Evie noted that the more Hesta spoke, the smoother and more melodious her tone. Each sound she made filled the world with the pureness of light.

She smiled. That she had been the one able to draw out such a sound filled Evie with a great deal of satisfaction, perhaps even a hint of happiness, too. She shook her head to clear her thoughts of such irrelevance.

Happiness did not figure in what she did. She was here to do as she was told, as she always did. She did not know this woman. Why should she be worried about how she sounded?

"You gave me your full name, yes, that is not the whole of it," Evie said.

At the sound of running feet storming up the stairs and along the passage outside, Hesta walked to the door and opened it.

Bethwood raced inside. He didn't look at Hesta, but almost pushed her aside so he could yell at Evie. "What the fuck is going on? What did you do?"

Evie hunched over herself and braced for pain as he raised his hand.

"Don't you dare!" Hesta shouted.

Bethwood froze in place, his arm prepared to strike and his mouth open.

"Don't you dare touch her, Godwyn Bethwood, not without speaking with me first. Just because I cannot always speak doesn't mean I'm stupid, or that you can race in here and do as you see fit. This is not your place."

He turned and grinned. "Hesta, she did it! You're cured!"

"Steady on, brother. This is not permanent. You know it isn't."

Brother? Evie thought. This lovely woman was his sister?

Bethwood started to bluster. "I know no such thing. Even if we have had limited success in the past, this is right. I feel it."

"Sit down, you oaf," Hesta said. She pointed at her armchair. "Sit there and don't move, don't speak, and don't interrupt."

He sat where instructed and smiled.

Hesta turned to Evie. "Evie, look at me. Look at my neck. What do you see?"

Evie did as she was bid. She spared a glance at Bethwood first, in case he had changed his mind and wanted to hit her.

"Ignore him," Hesta said.

"Scarring and the remains of the *infection* I removed."

"It's not a normal infection, though, is it, Evie?"

"No," she answered.

"Now focus your Gift again, think about what it felt like when you touched my skin, and concentrate on that."

"I can do that," Evie said. As she did, she saw something quite odd about Hesta's neck. Spots of light no larger than a pinhead flashed in and out of sight. "There is something happening. I didn't see it before. How could I have missed it?"

"And so, it goes on," Hesta said. "I will be mute by the morrow."

Bethwood slumped in Hesta's seat and leaned forward until he rested his head in his hands. "I thought we had it."

"This is the best so far. Maybe Evie will be able to remove it every time it gets bad."

Bethwood nodded. "I will bring her back."

"Let me talk to Evie first."

"She's mine. She will do as she is told."

"Godwyn, you will stop being such an ass and do things

my way." Hesta patted him on the shoulder. "Why don't you go downstairs and ask them to find the music for your favourite. I'll come down and sing. It would be nice to do that."

Bethwood smiled, and Evie had never seen such happiness on his face. "Of course. I will ready everyone, and we will wait for you."

Hesta closed the door on him as he left.

"You have questions, I think?"

Evie had to wonder if she was supposed to ask them. She had a use here, so that would help her standing at least.

"He's your brother? Your names are not the same."

"Hesta Estrallia is my stage name. Before I was known as Hesta Bethwood, even though Godwyn and I aren't related by birth. That's a long story for another time, and perhaps, given time, it is one I shall share."

"And do you own me, too, or am I still his property only?"

Hesta looked discomforted at that. "Sometimes needs must."

"Needs must? Needs must no matter the price that others must pay?"

"Sometimes, yes." As she spoke, she turned away. "Despair drives us to do many things."

Evie shook her head. Despair could never be used to describe Bethwood.

"Whatever you might think of us, it brought you to us. Is it wrong of me, of him, to want to take care of each other? We're family, and we were desperate." Hesta rose to her feet and walked over to one of the side tables. She lifted a cloth and brought out a tray filled with sweet rolls and savoury sandwiches. "I bet you're hungry, aren't you?"

"Yes," Evie said. "Avoiding free food when offered could be considered one of the many mortal sins for slaves. Especially when we're not often fed."

"Slave," Hesta said, as though the word had only just occurred to her. "Does Godwyn not feed you? Really?"

"Very rarely. We're kept in a stable, we lie on a stone floor with straw, and in the past, sometimes we were fed once a week." Evie stared at Hesta. She wanted her to know what life was like for them. She was rich and spoiled; she should share the consequences in some way. "But since I've had a use, we are fed more often, and that means Florie has a chance to live, but only so long as I do as I am told and earn him money."

Hesta offered her a plate covered with ham rolls, a slice of cheese, and a few pickles. Evie picked up one of the rolls and took a bite. She chewed and swallowed as fast as she could on the off chance that Hesta took the food back.

Hesta never touched the food but walked over to the window that faced the street. Evie recalled standing in a very similar position not so long back.

"He's not really a bad man, Evie. He needs to care for me, and he'll do anything to make sure I'm safe."

Evie decided not to comment. She ate her food and looked only at her plate. She wondered if she could wrap up some of the food and hide it for later.

Hesta turned around. "No matter what, it brought you to me, and I need you very much. Is that so very wrong of me?"

"To need someone's help? No. To make them a slave and abuse them. That is very wrong."

"Would you help me if I gave you your freedom?"

"And how much freedom would you give me?"

Hesta knelt down in front of Evie and took her hand. "I would give you anything you wanted to have your help."

"Would Bethwood—would Godwyn agree to this?"

"He would agree to anything I asked."

Right there, Evie guessed that the real power in the Bethwood family lay with Hesta.

"And I would teach you how to control your Gift. There is

more in you than you know, Evie, and I can teach you how to control it."

"So I would be *your* slave, then? Do *your* bidding at *your* whim?"

"No, you would be my companion, and you would live with me."

"Yet the chains would remain."

Hesta shook her head. "No, there would be no chains."

"Even if you dressed me in fine clothing, the chains, even if they were made of silk, are still chains."

"Evie—"

"How can I trust you when you have used and abused the Gifts of others?"

"Time would make you trust me eventually."

"I'll never trust any Bethwood for as long as I live," Evie said. "I am tired of all this, tired to my stomach. I don't—" Her eyes blurred, her head swam, and her stomach recoiled.

"Evie? Evie, what's wrong?" Hesta asked.

Evie couldn't answer as she felt herself slipping to the floor. Her body didn't respond to her control, her vision blackened and wavered. After that, she recalled nothing.

E vie woke up in a bed, a proper bed with soft sheets and a blanket. Two other things caught her attention. First of all, the smell was lovely. Fresh, sweet, and perfumed. The second was the music. Hesta was humming a tune as she bathed her head with a cool damp cloth.

"What happened?" Evie asked.

"You passed out. Are you all right now? You had me worried."

"I don't know." She moved her head to take in her surroundings. A bedroom. Softness against her hands. "Where am I?"

"You're in my bed," Hesta replied. "I was worried."

Evie lifted her hands from inside the covers and inspected her wrists.

"Evie?"

"No chains and no cuffs'" Evie replied.

"Of course not. Do you think I would chain you when you were weakest?"

Evie stared at her. "Your brother would."

"Well, I'm not he."

"No, I can see that."

Hesta smiled. "You know you have the most amazing eyes, and when you are angry, they glow brighter."

Evie snorted. "My eye colour is the least of my worries." She tried to sit up, but her head spun.

"Be careful. Let me get you a cup of sweet tea. I had some brought up for you."

"How long was I out?"

"Not long," Hesta said. She helped Evie to a sitting position and handed her a cup of tea.

"How long is not long?" Evie asked. She took a sip of the tea. Still hot, but not scalding.

"Ten minutes, perhaps a little longer. Do you know what happened?"

Evie shook her head. "No, do you?"

"I think it was because you healed me."

Evie thought that through. "Doing what I do is hard on the body sometimes, and it often saps my energy. That might be the reason."

Hesta brushed a strand of hair from Evie's face, and she smiled when Evie recoiled.

"I'll have to feed you up and take better care of you."

"I'm not one of your belongings. Not yet."

"Do you want to be?"

"Do I have a choice in the matter?"

Hesta patted her hand. "You have more power in this than you know. And I would not own you. Not now."

Evie stared into Hesta's brown eyes and wished she had one of those Gifts that could read minds. A part of her wanted to trust Hesta, and another part couldn't trust anyone as far as she could spit fire.

"You don't have to do anything. If you feel up to it, come downstairs. I'd like you to hear me sing. And I want to have a chat with Godwyn. You should be there for that, too. With Florie."

"Where is Florie?" Evie felt her cheeks heat and redden; she'd forgotten all about her.

Hesta laughed, and Evie loved the sound of her, like sunlight on water. "I think she is in one of the corridors learning how to juggle. At least, she was."

Evie smiled at that. Florie had come to no harm. "Sounds like Florie. She's still a child at heart."

"Will you come and hear me sing?"

What did she have to lose?

It did not take long for Evie to make herself presentable. As she did so, Hesta seemed quite ebullient and chatted of inconsequential issues, as though they had been friends for years.

The chatter continued until they were almost all the way to the backstage area.

"Do you know much about the theatre?" Hesta asked. She wrapped her scarf around her throat to hide the scarring and secured the cloth with a pin.

Evie shook her head. "It has not been a part of my social life since I was sold into slavery. And before that I hadn't been schooled much since I was too young."

"I'm sorry," Hesta said. She sounded so sincere that Evie almost believed her, but it would take more than one apology to make her forget her anger and frustrations.

Hesta touched her arm. "I'll show you around later, if you like. But first, there is something I must do."

The next thing Evie knew, Hesta pushed her against the

wall and held her there. She stared at Evie's lips, leaned a little closer, and kissed her full on the mouth.

Evie froze, her hands on the wall, her body refusing to move. "What the hell was that all about?" she asked.

"Sorry about that, but you'll thank me." She smiled. "Actually, I'm not at all sorry."

"I will thank you?"

"Yes." Hesta gestured along the corridor. "Shall we continue? In my defence, that was far faster than trying to get you to understand." She touched her lips. "Nice, too, even if you weren't trying."

"You arrogant, spoilt, rich tart. I may only be a slave to you. But I have my principles, and I'm no whore."

Hesta looked shocked.

"What did you expect, taking a liberty like that?"

Hesta's cheeks reddened. "I'm sorry. But really, this is the best way. Give me an hour."

"Do I have a choice?" Evie folded her arms over her chest and glared at her. "Very well. Show me what difference an hour will make. But I can tell you, force yourself on me like that again, and I will find a way to kill you."

"Thank you," Hesta said, obviously ignoring the part where Evie threatened to kill her. "You'll not regret trusting me."

"I don't trust you."

"You will one day."

Evie shook her head, exasperated.

"Come on," Hesta said. "Let me show you what this is all about."

Inside the theatre, a great many people now sat upon the rows of seating. The musicians played their tuning cacophony and several people on stage flounced about as though they had some place to be but were not sure where it was. To Evie, chaos seemed the order of the day.

The moment they entered the room, people stopped

moving, the musicians stopped making their din, and silence descended.

"You ought to sit on the stage, listen to the song, and watch the audience," Hesta said.

"Why?"

"You'll see. It will mean more in the end, I promise."

Evie shrugged and allowed Hesta to guide her to a suitable spot.

"From here, you can see me and you can see them, too," she said.

"Is that important?" Evie asked.

Bethwood approached them on the edge of the stage. "There you are. Wondered where you were. Or if I'd dreamed it."

Hesta smiled. "No dream. I am here now, are you ready? Have you chosen your song?"

Bethwood grinned. "The Wild Gardens of Kilarrie," he said. "Is that all right?"

"Of course. I thought you might choose that one," she said.

He turned to the musicians. "Ready yourself."

Evie felt a hand on her shoulder, and when she turned, Hesta scrutinised her face, as though searching for something. Evie stared back into her brown eyes and nodded. "I'll listen," she said.

Bethwood escorted Hesta to the centre of the stage. He acted in an attentive manner, as though he thought Hesta a most fragile creature. She looked over her shoulder at Evie and winked.

Hesta stood in the middle of the stage and opened her arms. "It's been a while, my friends. Shall we stretch the music?"

A round of enthusiastic applause filled the room. The sheer enthusiasm of the people gathered stirred Evie from her anger. She could sense great warmth from everyone, and it didn't fit with her experience of the Bethwoods. Then again, she was a slave; no one cared if she thought well of them.

Hesta took a few deep breaths and nodded. Silence once more dominated, and when a chap in shirt and trousers tapped a thin stick against a lectern, the sound echoed throughout the entire room.

Evie's first thought was to watch the audience. Every single one sat at the front of their seat, gazing at Hesta with a longing so deep it almost had depth. Of those in the room, not a single one looked any place other than at Hesta.

The music began. It was a slow piece, slow enough that Hesta began to sway on the spot. She moved with such grace and fluidity that Evie forgot about the audience. Hesta returned her gaze and began to sing.

The sound that came from her mouth could only be described as divine. Evie knew nothing about music, but this song filled her with such happiness she felt she could burst with pleasure.

Hesta walked towards her.

'Look at the audience.' The words filled her mind. She moved her attention as directed, and noticed the people as though for the first time. One by one, the musicians stopped playing. The man with the stick stared up at Hesta, his eyes focused on her.

Hesta sang on. Her voice soared into the heavens and came back as though touched by angels. Every inch of the theatre echoed with the beauty of her music. It was, Evie decided, the sort of voice that could stop an army in its tracks.

When she took in the rest of the audience, she realised it wasn't only the musicians who were smitten by Hesta's voice. Every one of the people watching, without exception, stared at Hesta with an almost slack-jawed, blank expression. Every single one of them.

Evie jumped off the stage and wandered around along the

first row. She stood in front of a stage hand, and as she blocked his view, he growled and pushed her out of the way.

Inside the pit, the musicians all stood, their instruments held in slack hands, and their faces turned to Hesta in glassy-eyed adoration.

When the song ended, Hesta stood at the edge of the stage, her arms out. She spoke to the audience, her voice clear, and every word echoed through the room as though it were music all on its own. "I know you will do everything you can to make this a regular occurrence," she said to the whole audience. She turned to Evie. "You'll help me?"

"Hesta—" Evie started.

Hesta held a finger to her lips. "Remember, there is only one woman in the entire city who sings like I do. Remember and never forget it."

The audience began to move. They smiled, they clapped, they cheered.

"It has been a while. Was I any good?" Hesta called out.

"You're as brilliant as ever," Godwyn said.

Hesta gestured Bethwood over. "I think you should gift Evie to me, Godwyn. I couldn't have done it without you or her."

"Of course. She is yours," he replied.

"And I think we need young Florie, too. She would be vital for the stage lighting," Hesta added.

"If you need her, yes. She is yours."

Hesta smiled. "Godwyn, if Evie is going to help me, we can start to get the audiences back, don't you think?"

"That would be lovely," he replied.

"She needs clothing and money," Hesta said.

"Whatever she wants and needs," he replied.

Evie's mouth opened in surprise. Like the others, Bethwood leaned forward in his seat, his eyes wide and glassy, a broad grin on his face.

Hesta stepped close to her and, with gentle fingers, lifted Evie's jaw to close her mouth. *'Don't be surprised.'*

Then she turned away and addressed the room again. "Thank you for your kindness. I think we should add a little singing to the upcoming performances, don't you?"

"Yes!" they answered in one resounding roar. "Yes!"

Hesta pointed to a young man in breeches and a plain shirt. "Pieter, please show Florie what you know about lamps and starting fires, and if Florie likes it, she can help you."

"Yes, ma'am," he replied.

"Can I do that?" Florie asked.

Evie smiled. "Of course you can. Go, enjoy the theatre."

Hesta took Evie's hand. "Now will you listen to me?"

Evie nodded, and they left the people of the theatre to their work.

14

———————

E vie stood at the window in Hesta's room and stared outside. Her thoughts were a jumble. "What the hell just happened?"

"You have your Gift, Evie, that was mine."

Evie turned around but found herself distracted by the sad look on Hesta's face.

"Should I be scared of you?"

"No, never fear me. You of all people should not fear me."

"What are you?

"I'm a siren."

"Seriously? A siren is a creature that lures sailors to their deaths."

Hesta laughed, but there was little humour in the sound. "Some sirens might, but not me. Most of what a siren might do is myth."

"Myth or not, if you don't lure them to their deaths, you want to control people."

"Sometimes. When I sing, I can invoke any emotion I want in those who hear me. I can charm people, make them do my will by twisting any idea to sound like a good one."

"I know that. I saw the effect you can have on people."

"It is who I am. I sing to them and—"

"You control them."

Hesta didn't answer out loud, but she managed a nod.

"I'm a slave, and you can enslave people with your voice. Of course I'm scared of you. You could make me *want* to be your slave."

"I wouldn't do that to you."

"Why not?"

Hesta stood next to the door, as though she was the one who might run. "I sang, yes, that is my Gift. And I gave you my kiss. For a while, that makes you immune." Hesta unwrapped the scarf and draped it over the back of her chair.

"So, the only way I can keep my mind is to keep kissing you?"

The side of Hesta's mouth rose in a small smirk. "Pleasing though that may be, I'll not take kisses from someone who has no wish to give them. You're safe."

"Good." Evie turned back to the window. Outside, people trudged along the street, unaware of the magics present in this building.

Hesta took a step closer. Evie could see her reflection in the window as she reached out, then changed her mind.

"Are you mad at me?" she asked instead. "Godwyn has granted you freedom."

"Freedom? What freedom? He gave me to you." Evie leaned against the wall and rubbed the bridge of her nose. "Really, what the hell is this about?"

"It's very complicated, Evie."

"Does Bethwood know what you can do?"

"No. I kept my skill hidden, and that worked fine for a while. We kept our performances private, small, so we could make a quiet impact on people we wished to impress."

"You mean, you controlled people to get your own way," Evie said.

"A little maybe. I like to think that I offered a quiet and gentle influence."

"Right."

Hesta shook her head. "Then he forgot what we were doing and thought it would be better to bring in as many as we could."

Evie turned. "You control Bethwood."

"I did, for a while."

Evie couldn't stop her voice from rising. A lifetime of misery fueled her anger. "You made him do all these things he does? You made him enslave the Gifted? Why the hell would you do that?"

Hesta sighed. "Because I must. You understand, Evie, when the world is against you, you have to do everything you can to survive. You know that. The powerless and the poor must do what they can to get by. I have done no more than I had to."

"But how could you do it like this? By enslaving people?" Evie asked.

"It is what I do, Evie. My skill is to bend people to my will."

Evie let her thoughts drift for a moment. "Your throat. You couldn't speak."

"And my chances for using the full range of my skills have been held in abeyance."

"So, how long has Bethwood been independent of your control?"

"It's been a few years," Hesta admitted. "I started all this by needing help."

"How did it start, then?"

Hesta smiled. "I made a name for myself in the theatre, and we attended a number of private groups. Groups of very influential people, which gave us, and Godwyn, access to money and power."

"And now he is on his own and twisting it his way," Evie said.

"I gave him power when I sang, and now he has used that power to achieve his goals…our goals."

"Which are?"

"To live in comfort and poverty free. To live without fear of persecution, or violence."

"This is the life for all gifted."

"Not all. But most of all I want to be free of pain."

Evie turned her attention from the window and back to Hesta. "Your throat and the sickness. When I thought of it as a curse, it made more sense to me." Evie paused to gather her thoughts. "I thought it looked like a handprint. It is a hand, isn't it?" She tried to step back, but the wall got in the way. "It's a bloody handprint. What the hell burns and curses like that?"

"Many things are capable of this, Evie. If you want to know more, I will tell you everything I know."

"I'm not sure what to believe, or if I can trust anything you say."

"I'm sorry, but I was desperate. And Godwyn was distraught." She sighed, and it sounded so heartfelt that Evie felt her anger diminish a little. She knew she would also do whatever she needed to survive.

"This slavery of the Gifted is not the way to do it. You know that, don't you?"

Hesta nodded. "I didn't know he'd gone so far. I'm sorry."

Evie stared at Hesta's neck.

"What's the matter?"

Evie narrowed her eyes. "Your neck."

"Bugger. It's starting to glow, isn't it?"

Evie nodded. "I can see it. Like tiny bursts of light."

"Keep back, Evie. I don't want you to be in the way of what happens next."

"What do you mean by that?" Evie sniffed the air. "What's that smell?"

Hesta sniffed with her. "Oh, shit," she said.

A burst of smoke erupted from the floor and solidified into a man. Well, something man-shaped, although Evie had never seen a man who looked like this.

He wore no clothing, and his skin had been replaced with something more akin to burning coals or molten rock. Dark on the outside, blazing with heat and fire underneath. Two tiny protrusions at the top of his head curled up like horns and glinted with purple light.

"You were told," he said in a voice that rumbled like rock grinding against rock. "The price to be paid, siren, is the loss of your voice. You are an afront to my Prince Sasaan Isck for the insult to his daughters, Polula, Mistress of Poison, Evaline, the Lady Blight, and Ostrana, the Queen of Pestilence. You have failed to do as commanded and the cost of your impertinence is, as it was then, your voice."

He stepped forward and gripped Hesta around the throat. The smell of burning and singeing skin grew stronger. "Be thankful I only take your voice, when it would be better to rip out your throat and be done with you."

As the burning hand closed around Hesta's neck, she tried to cry out, but it sounded more like a screech.

"No!" Evie screamed.

The creature turned around to regard Evie with flaming eyes. "Go, or I will add you to what I take back," he rumbled. "Or I'll burn you until nothing more than ash remains at my feet."

Undeterred by his threats, Evie did not back down.

"Leave her alone." She didn't think about the danger they were all in. The heat radiating from his skin like the blast from an opened furnace meant nothing. Yes, it would hurt, it always hurt, but it would heal. It always healed, and this would be no different she decided, and rushed forward. She paused before she touched this man of burning lava. The fear of pain made her hesitate. But she grabbed his shoulder regardless. She wouldn't be able to pull him away if she didn't risk a burn or two.

When her hand touched him, pain blasted across her flesh. Searing agony raced through every fibre of her hand, along her arm, until it exploded inside her mind. It was worse than anything she'd ever experienced. Worse than being branded, worse even than anything she could have imagined. For a moment, Evie thought she had placed her hand inside a furnace. She could think of nothing but fire and burning. She could smell her skin burning and crisp with the heat of it. It was all too much. She screamed in agony.

'No, Evie, no,' echoed inside her thoughts. '*He'll kill you.*'

And then it changed. A wave of cold rushed through her and overwhelmed the heat.

Her scream of pain became a cry of defiance. "No!" she roared.

The pain stopped. The burning ceased to be a consideration. Ice gathered at her finger tips, and her Gift called to all that she was. What she was, she decided, was something uncertain. Different. She wiped her face with her free hand. Roughness, like crushed glass, ground under her fingers. Crystals of ice brushed from her face, fell to the ground in glittering shards.

"What in all the Thirteen Thrones of the Underworld is this?" the fiery demon cried.

An indescribable force tore through the whole of Evie's body, and will alone kept her together. Blazing heat and freezing cold raged and fought until she felt herself at the heart of some maelstrom of opposing forces.

Black ice crept over her hands and arms. It tickled as it grew across her skin, and the incongruity of such powers tickling her almost made her grin at the inappropriateness of it all.

Evie gripped his shoulder with one blacked, icy hand. He flinched at the contact. He smoldered and smoked where she touched him.

"No. This can't be. There are no more syphons. This is not poss—"

The being imploded in a pile of cinders and ash. The ice from her hands shredded away from her skin and tinkled as it hit the floor.

Evie stared at her ordinary hands, which no longer showed any signs of the black ice. "What happened?"

Hesta flew at her and enveloped Evie in a tight embrace. "Evie, you did it! You saved me."

"What did I do?"

"Everything," Hesta replied. She kissed Evie on the cheek.

"You have a thing for kissing me, Hesta Bethwood."

"How could I not?"

"You could restrain yourself," she said distractedly. Now that the action was over, the fear and terror came crashing down on her. She shook so hard her knees almost gave way. She recalled the horror of all she had seen, the feel of the creature against her skin. The memory of burning seared into her mind, and she could see nothing but her own skin blackening.

Shock had her in its grip, and she could do nothing to keep herself upright. Hesta's slender arms enfolded her more tightly and held her on her feet. Before she knew it, she'd wrapped her arms around Hesta and hugged her back.

"Are you all right?"

Evie couldn't answer. When she considered that she had tussled with a demon, maybe even destroyed it, she shook all over again.

"It'll be all right," Hesta said.

For the moment, no matter her anger and distrust of Hesta and Godwyn, she could not turn away from the comfort of this closeness. It took her a while to find her voice, and when she did, she stepped back from the contact.

"What's going on, Hesta? I think I should know now. And what did I do to that thing?"

Hesta pulled away and helped herself to the jug of water. She poured a little over the place where the flaming man had stood. That the carpet had been scorched could not be changed, but the water would help make sure the rug did not burst into flame. She sat in her chair and reached for Evie.

"What do you think you did to him?"

"I don't know."

"Think about what you felt at the time."

"Anger," Evie said. "I saw him grab hold of you, and I felt angry enough to intervene."

"Weren't you scared of the burning?"

"Yes." Evie shook her head. "It hurts, but I can't be marked by fire. It's just pain. I can deal with that."

Hesta frowned. "Just pain, indeed. How can touching a demon like him just be simple pain?"

Evie shrugged. "As I touched him, my Gift responded, but in a way I never knew it could."

"I knew you were a special healer the moment Godwyn told me about you."

"I'm not a healer, though, am I?" Evie said.

"I don't think so. He called you a syphon. What does that mean?" Hesta froze. "Did you absorb him? Do you need to purge?"

Evie thought for a moment, then shook her head. "No, I took from him and fed it back. But not quite. He burned. I was like ice. I think I sent him back to where he came from."

"Are you sure?

"I've no idea. But he went somewhere."

"Or you destroyed him," Hesta said.

"Hesta, what was he?"

"That was a herald of the Underworld. Sasaan Isck is a

Prince of the Poison Waters, one of the thirteen thrones of the Underworld, and I offended one of his daughters."

"How?"

"Oh, that's a long story, and I'm not proud of it."

"You want my trust, and yet you will not tell me what the hell is going on! That isn't fair." Evie's temper grew until she could no longer restrain herself. "Because of you, Godwyn enslaved me and others, and now I've met this damned beast from I don't know where–"

"From Hell, or the Underworld. Take your pick," Hesta interrupted.

Evie glared at Hesta for a moment. "Some hell beast appeared in front of me. I could have been hurt, killed, or taken to wherever he was from. Don't you think you owe me an explanation at the very least?"

Hesta sighed and turned away. "You're right, I'm sorry."

"Sorry isn't enough."

"Let me explain." Hesta wrapped her arms around herself and took a deep breath. "They're angry with me, the Princes of Hell, because I wouldn't take one of their daughters as my lover. None of the thrones of hell, nor their spawn, like to have their wishes thwarted. So it seems to me."

Evie felt her cheeks burn, and she focussed her gaze on the floor. "Oh. I mean, how did you become involved with the thrones and princes of the Underworld?"

"It wasn't my choice. They seek any and all Gifted people. Some skills are more valued than others. Sirens are a valued addition for any of the thrones."

"Thrones?"

Hesta stared out the window, but she didn't seem to be aware of anything in this room. If anything, she adopted a dreamy, faraway mien, as though she were scanning through her memories. "As I said, there are thirteen thrones to Hell. The King is the Over-Throne, and there are twelve princes who each have their own domain."

"I see," Evie said.

"Anyway, once a prince knows of you, it is difficult to shake them off." She sighed. "It started not long after I discovered by gift. I found a demon of some kind harassing a group of women working at a hat shop, so I helped them."

"What did you do?"

"I made them feel more powerful than the demon, and when they were no longer scared of the creature, it had to leave." She grinned. "That, and the fact that I sang and caused it great pain."

"Brave you."

"Not really. I was young, foolish, and proud, but it helped the women."

"Then what happened?" Evie asked.

"They sent a different demon to see me. A herald, like the one you saw, but this one tried to take me to the Underworld, or Hell. They said I must go to them, and I had an obligation to go, but I refused."

"Well, goodness," Evie said. "I didn't think Hell was a real place."

"I wish. Take this as your welcome to the worlds beyond."

Evie shook her head. "I'd rather not."

"Are you still angry with me?" Hesta asked. Her voice dropped and smoothed out.

"Are you trying to sway me with your voice?"

Hesta reached out and took Evie's hands in hers. Warm fingers brushed across her skin and soothed her somehow.

"No. You have my kiss, and that is like having my favour so I can't control you." Hesta smiled. "He called you a syphon, and now I am not sure I could have affected you anyway."

"What is a syphon?"

"In truth, I'm not sure. I would guess that you take from one place and send it elsewhere. You take sickness from a person and empty the corruption someplace else. You can pass it on to other people, too."

"That's how I think it works. I thought my skill was like a sponge, but syphon is better."

"Will you stay with me? I need your help, Evie, and now that they know you exist, they might come after you, too. We could learn about your Gift. There must be someone who knows more about it."

Evie sat and regarded Hesta's hands holding hers. "I don't know."

"You are free to go, you know. I wouldn't want to keep you here with me if you didn't want to stay."

Evie squeezed Hesta's hands. "Maybe two minds thinking about things will be better than one. We could work together."

"I would like that."

"There is one thing—actually a couple of conditions."

"All right, name them."

"If I wish to leave, I can. Florie, too."

"Granted."

"Two, if anyone asks for our help, no matter who they are, we help them if we can."

Hesta looked thoughtful. "All right, that as well. You stay as long as you want, and we will help whoever needs our help." She smiled. "It would be a kind of recompense for all the hardship I have caused you and others."

Evie nodded. "I would like that. But know this, I'm not your slave."

Hesta let go of Evie so she could open one of the drawers in her bureau. She pulled out a bulging purse and handed it to her. "Take this. Take Florie, and go wherever you want to go. I would love for you to stay here, but if you want to leave Bristelle, or even leave the Angles, I would never stop you."

Evie opened the purse and started, open-mouthed, at the contents. "There is a fortune here."

Hesta shrugged. "It's all I have, but it should be enough to get you started. You're no one's slave, Evie Chester. Never again will anyone put chains of any sort upon you. You have my word."

Evie didn't know what to say, but in her heart she remembered the promise she'd made to Florie.

They *had* survived, and they were free.

I hope you have enjoyed this story. If you did, please consider leaving an honest review. Most of all, I just want to know that you have enjoyed the story.

Thank you

If you want to know more about new books, background details and information not printed any place else, then subscribe to the reader's list.

https://www.subscribepage.com/nitaround

Visit my website at
www.nitaround.com

Or join my facebook group

www.facebook.com/groups/nitaroundbooks/

ACKNOWLEDGMENTS

Many thanks to everyone that helped to make this story possible. Krista's editing, Amy's beta reading and story development, with May Dawney's fantastic covers, and this all adds up into something special. I appreciate the work and skills each of you have. I couldn't do it without you.

For me, the most important of all, are the readers. If you enjoyed reading my stories please leave a review. This is the lifeblood of an author, and we cherish the days when a reader leaves a kind word. Trust me, it goes a long way, and sometimes it is all that keeps us going. For reviewers everywhere, thank you.

The Towers of the Earth

Prequel: A Pinch of Salt
Prequel: A Hint of Hope

Book 1: A Touch of Truth
Book 2: A Touch of Rage
Book 3: A Touch of Darkness
Book 4: A Touch of Ice

The Evie Chester Files:

Case 1: Lost and Found
Case 2: Sirens and Syphons
Case 3: Fur and Fangs

Other Books:
The Ghost of Emily Tapper

Sapphic Romance as Encarnita Round
Fresh Start

Printed in Great Britain
by Amazon

82533513R00120